Awakening to You

TRILOGY

FIFI FLOWERS

Champagne Girl Studio

Cover Design by LKO Designs
Formatting by BB eBooks
Edited by Jacquelyn Ayres

Published by Champagne Girl Studios

www.FifiFlowers.com

Other Books by Fifi Flowers
A Window to Love, (Book 1, Windows Series)
Reclining Nude in Chicago, (Book 1, Encounters Series)

TABLE OF CONTENTS

Acknowledgements

Time to say "merci" to a few people…

To ma maman, *thank you* doesn't seem like the right words for you, what you do for me is incredible… I love you!

Gigeebelle, mon amie, thank you for taming me in more ways than one… I love what you do to me!

Thank you to all of my friendly betareaders that do so much more than just read my books, they support you give me is spectacular: Lilah, Jeanette, Amy, and Andrea thanks for loving my characters as much as I did. I'm feeling like all of you—sad to walk away from Sofie and Drake's Awakening to You story. A special thanks to Kim, I love when my phone chimes with the word, "bonjour," you always brighten my day!

Jacquelyn, my editor extraordinaire, thank you, thank you. It has been a pleasure to work with you on this series. I look forward to reading and laughing at your comments on future books.

Paul at BB ebooks Formatting, thank you for your amazing speed, expertise, and kindness.

Sassy Queens of Tease & Design, thank you for all of your support. Becca and Angel, I love all of the wonderful banners and teasers you have created for this series. Stracey, thank you so much for spreading my name everywhere, along with making FAB swag.

Nelle L'Amour, thank you for your encouragement. It is a delight knowing you. I enjoy our conversations immensely.

Thank you to all Book Bloggers that have made this series more visible, your support is truly, truly appreciated more than you could ever know. Some key bloggers, I must thank for going beyond: Bets of Cover to Cover Book Blog, thank you for all of your help from readings to teasers to promoting, and pushing me to finish. Shannon of Book Boyfriend Reviews, thank you for hosting my cover reveals and releases, along with loving Drake. Thank you Lizzy for going above and beyond the call of duty, love this beautiful cover! Samatha of Naughty Books and Bits, thank you for your unending support. Thank you to Michele, for helping me with Reading is Fashionable, you allow me more time to write. Claire and Wendy of Bare Naked Words, thank you for putting together the Awakening to You Trilogy book tour, and sharing my promos. Ebony of E. McMillan: Author Support, thank you for helping me.

And to everyone on my *Fabulous with Fifi Street Team* thank you for sharing my book promos and me with the book world. BIG MWAHs to each and every one of you.

Awakening

to You...

in Boston

FIFI FLOWERS

Champagne Girl Studio

Chapter One

Y AWNING, I OPENED my eyes to the brightness that filled my hotel suite. Stretching out in my empty king-size bed, "mmmm... sunshine... divine," I said to no one but myself as I untangled my surprisingly sore body from a mass of twisted high-count Egyptian cotton sheets. I must've had some good dreams or nightmares throughout my slumber that caused me to toss and turn, entwining my body within the bed linens. I remembered that I had plenty of wine last night, but apparently not enough to drag a hard body home with me.

Deciding against having my usual continental breakfast: coffee, fruit, and pastry, via room service, I got out of bed and headed for the bathroom. Looking in the mirror, crazy, dark, honey-blonde hair and smudged makeup under my green, bloodshot eyes reflected back at me. Recollection of the night before's events wandered into my mind. Aah, yes... there was a lot of wild dancing and pretty little glasses, filled with bright lime liquid, lined up on a long, wooden bar. Reaching into the shower stall, I regulated the water, shrugged off my tank top and panties. Stepping under the steamy hot spray, the pulsating water soothed my aching body. I was quite thankful I didn't have a beast of a headache as my fingers danced through my hair, pulling out the many snarls. Once I was squeaky clean and dried off, I brushed my teeth, applied little mascara, burnt-raspberry lipstick, and sunscreen. Then I put on my favorite McQueen floral print skirt, white fitted, ribbed-cotton t-shirt, and tan, multi-strapped, flat sandals.

Grabbing my bag filled with all my necessary designing tools, I exited my room. Bending down, I scooped up The Boston Globe off the carpet outside my door, tucked it under my arm, and strode down the long hall to the elevator. I often walked down the nine flights of stairs but that morning my tender feet screamed, "No!" Popping out of the elevator, I was tempted to slide down the brass railing, attached to five shorts steps, but was not inclined to show off my pale pink thong; instead, I bounced down the stairs. Smiling, I strolled through the lobby, waved at the front desk clerks, and winked at the concierge as I passed his desk to make my way out the front door. "Good morning," I said to the doorman as he quickly pulled the door open for me. I then turned left toward the Commons.

My occupation as a set designer brought me to theatre district in the fabulous the city of Boston; the Shubert Theatre, next to my hotel, specifically. Fortunately for me, the project was during the warmer months as I have never been fond of cold weather. Let me re-phrase that. I was not a fan of freezing, bitter, cold-to-the-bone weather for an extended period of time. Yes, I was always up for a weekend or week long ski vacation, but day in and day out coldness; no thank you. Late spring, summer, and early fall was the longest amount of time I could ever imagine myself living in Beantown. Well, I must admit that I may be willing to spend a week in Boston during the winter to experience ice skating on the Frog pond. The thought of watching people bundled up and sledding down snowy embankments in the Commons was a charming vision. I guess the key word for me was *visit,* not live. However, as I made my way along Boylston Street, across from the park, I thought if only the weather on this particular summer day was like this year round; I could live here.

Crossing the street at Arlington, I turned left down Newbury Street and found a quaint, little coffee shop complete with an older, attractive waitress, wearing a starched uniform and an up-do hairstyle. She called me "Honeybee." Sitting at a table near the window with the sun warming me, I ordered coffee and a brie and chive omelette with sourdough toast before I opened the paper to the theatre section. I was never one to shy away from reviews.

The evening before was the opening night for a show I was involved with that was scheduled to run for six weeks. The original production had debuted on Broadway and due to its great success, a few smaller companies began taking the show on the road. I didn't normally work in theatre; I preferred movies and cable TV series. I agreed to this job as a favor to Tamber

Marshall, a fellow set designer, who had to back out of it at the last minute. Besides, how can you refuse a man singing Dave Loggins' 1974 hit song, *Please Come to Boston,* to you? I loved Boston in springtime and familiar with the play and my friend's initial designs, I easily stepped in to complete the tasks at hand. Beginning mid-May along with a play crew, we infiltrated a warehouse to build moveable set pieces and stitch costumes that would be installed and worn in the theatre within a month's time, when rehearsals began. One of my favorite parts of this gig was that I could walk everywhere and take in the glorious sights of the city.

After breakfast, I window shopped my way down the street until I crossed over through the gates and into the botanical area of the Public Garden. Walking by a bronze statue of President Washington seated proudly upon a horse I said, "Hello, George," and continued through the various plants and flowers that decorated the area. When I first arrived in Boston almost two months ago, the tulips were shooting up and opening to their current perfect cup-shape status. Oh how I loved tulips. They might be my all-time favorite bloom. Moving on to the middle of the park, I arrived at the lagoon where large swan boats were inhabited by tourist being pedal around by young college students. Besides boats adorned with big white swans, I learned that two beautiful, live, white swans were brought to the lagoon to reside during the warm months. Ha! Good weather visitors like me. Crossing over a beautiful expansion bridge, I could see children feeding and chasing real ducks along the banks and heard parents yelling, "Leave them alone!" Smiling to myself, I strolled farther down the path to see other kids having their pictures snapped while they sat on one of the eight brass ducklings and their mother. I loved seeing the charming "Make Room for Ducklings" installation from Robert McCloskey's book by the same name.

Exiting the park at the corner of Beacon Street and Charles Street, I popped into a well-known coffee establishment and purchased an iced vanilla bean cafe latte before continuing my stroll through the Commons. With a cool beverage in my hand, I promenaded along the footpath to the Frog Pond. Such a happy place. I was lucky to find an empty bench bathed in sunlight. Parked at the far end of the pond near the baseball fields, I listened to the delightful laughs of children of all ages playing and splashing in the watering hole. Looking around, I saw happy faces and dirty faces painted with ice cream, ketchup, mustard... remnants of snack bar cuisine. Then I saw a face that caused me to stare.

A tall, dark-haired man, sporting a custom fit, slate-blue suit that nicely complimented his body, walked into the area. With a cellphone to his ear, he sat down on a bench in perfect view. Slipping off his jacket, he neatly folded it up and holding his phone with his shoulder, he rolled up his shirt sleeves. He had equally beautiful, muscular biceps to match his face. I couldn't look away. I was entranced and happy he was so wrapped up in a phone conversation that I could continue my perusal of his lean, hard body, narrow hips, broad shoulders and the way his legs filled his tailored pants. I licked my lips, imagining what might lie beneath those clothes that looked so out of place at the Frog Pond in comparison to the swimsuits and summer clothing of the rest of the inhabitants. And that was when I was caught.

Our eyes locked. I couldn't look away. My breathing became irregular. If not for the shrill of my cellphone, I may have hyperventilated. Looking down, I lifted my bag and began rummaging around inside of what I always called, "the black hole." Marco Zitti, the stage manager's name flashed on my screen. I knew I needed to answer. Sliding my finger across the screen before bringing the phone to my ear, I looked up to see an empty bench. I gazed around but not a suited, hot man was to be found so I turned my attention to the already ranting artist. I was relieved he was just calling me to blow off some steam and assured me that I did not have to go into the theatre. Marco was having one of his typical meltdowns when people did not see things his way. I always seemed to be his sounding board. Once he got whatever was on his mind out, calmness returned. Thankfully, the situation turned out to be another one of his dramatic moments. I was thrilled that he could handle everything because I could really use a night off. The lack of sleep, the excess of libations from the night before, and sitting in the sun had begun to affect me. Casting my eyes around one last time, I shoved my belongings back into my black nylon messenger bag and stood to leave.

Heading back to my temporary home on Tremont, I stopped by my neighborhood flower shop and was greeted by the two lovely owners. The beautiful red-headed Betsy was busily working while a cute, petite, platinum and black-streaked Iris purred multiple suggestions in her direction. The Boston Flowergirls shop sat on the corner of Boylston and Charles Street in a brick-front building. I loved how they displayed ready-to-purchase flower bouquets in plastic buckets wrapped with white picket fencing under a green and white striped awning. I happily plucked one or two arrangements to carry home weekly; they enhanced and, on occasion, perfumed my hotel suite. With my flower selection entwined with string and slipped into a plastic sleeve, I bid the ladies a lovely evening and went in search of dinner.

Turning the corner onto my street, I was instantly hit by the smell of pepperoni, garlic, and gooey mozzarella cheese, lofting through the air. Yum! Popping into a friendly wine shop first, I gave in to a bottle of Chianti, calling my name and then made a beeline for New York Style Pizza. Back in my room, I tossed the small pizza box on the bed, kicked off my shoes, changed into lounge wear, and poured a tumbler glass full of wine. Turning on the TV, I watched medieval characters eat, fight, and fuck. My thoughts ran to Mr. Suit in the park. Who was he? Was he in the park to meet his wife… and children? Would he return? Would I see him again? I was uncertain, but I had to know.

Chapter Two

D URING THE NEXT couple weeks, I worked during
the day with fellow theatre production people,
making sure all visual elements were ready for each
performance; matinees and evenings. Once I was finished
for the day, I usually strolled around the city. Boston, as
far as I was concerned, was one of the best cities to
explore. History could be found on just about every
corner. I loved to follow the Freedom Trail; the red
painted line that wandered around the city streets from
one historical landmark to another. There was so much
to see along the way from the Commons to Bunker Hill
Monument across the Charles River. Back home, I
would never venture into a cemetery. But one day, I
found myself reading various grave markers in the
Granary Burying Grounds, including one that marked
Paul Revere's resting place. Another feature to my daily
walks was a little peeking (I liked the word "peeking"
rather than stalking) of the Frog Pond. Of course, I was
looking for a certain someone but I also enjoyed the
noise before making my way back to a quiet room.

To my delight, the beautiful, suited man could often
be found next to the watering hole; some days he was

already at the pond when I arrived, while other days he came strutting up. My body had the usual reaction: heart pounding, nipples pebbled, panties wet, and core throbbing whenever he looked my way. I wondered what would happen to me if he actually touched me. *Would I melt? Would I spontaneously burst? Ignite?* He set me on fire with just his gaze and his brief grins, when he caught me sneaking glimpses of him.

One day, he was already at the pond with his jacket off and folded on a bench, his shirt sleeves rolled up, as well as his pant legs, and he was wading in the water. I smiled when he looked my direction and he returned my expression. I thought he was about to walk my way when a woman joined him in the water. She began speaking to him. She didn't look his type, but how could I know his type? I didn't even know him. As they continued to converse in a jovial manner, they were joined by a small child. I didn't need to see anymore, I turned away to head home with my heart aching. It appeared he belonged to another and I couldn't bear to watch. I decided to stay away from the pond for a few days, but it didn't take long before I was dying for a Mr. Suit fix. Fortunately, I was not disappointed.

There he was; gorgeous and alone. Not a child, nor a woman, was near him as he sat on his usual bench, talking on his phone. I took a seat on a bench not far from him and busied myself with my tablet. It felt like his eyes were burning into me and when I looked up, he was looking my way. I swallowed hard as I watched him stand and take steps in my direction. "Oh my, he's coming to talk to me," I thought as I shamelessly stared at his hard, taut body, sauntering over. Suddenly, the moment was lost. Two little boys suddenly approached me, splashing and laughing. Out of the corner of my eye, I could see that he had stopped dead in his tracks. I desperately wanted to say something to him... wave maybe... but my attention turned to the little creatures, insisting on getting me drenched. One was apologizing while the other one continued to giggle and flick water. "He thinks you're pretty," the younger one said and the older one was quick to retort, "No, I don't. He thinks you look like Sleeping Beauty." I laughed at their bantering and then they both began chatting away, telling me stories while I listened to them; bemused. Looking away from my two young suitors, I glanced in the suit's direction and he smiled, then grabbed his jacket from the bench and with his head down, he walked off. Sadly, I watched him until I felt a tug on my skirt and I turned to my admirers, briefly. When I looked up again, he had vanished. Damn, I wouldn't get another chance until Monday.

Over the weekend, I entertained a director friend of mine and his wife. He wanted to discuss a possible production design opportunity. Since graduating from film school, I had submitted my resume along with work samples to various projects. So far, most attempts at production design jobs had been filled. Filled by men because this field was still dominated by *the boys club*. I just needed the right film. I had great concepts all figured out for this project. It was meant for me; it was my chance to shine. It looked like this was practically mine. However, I knew David would not just hand it to me. I spent the next few days researching, studying, sketching, along with overseeing my theatre gig. I never got a chance to do a little *sightseeing* in The Commons.

After my director pal left on Tuesday afternoon, I decided to pop over to the pond for an ice cream. Who was I kidding? Yes, I wanted a sweet treat alright but a Popsicle was not exactly what I envisioned in my mouth. I laughed, "Good excuse, Sofie." However, the laughter stopped when no suit appeared and I found myself standing in the snack shack line, chatting with a woman who also seemed defeated. I had hoped she wasn't looking for *my man* as I grabbed my ice cream from the snack stand vendor and said goodbye.

The next day, after working on a few amateur architectural sketches, I decided to take a tour of the Prescott House, on Beacon Street, across from the Frog Pond. Of course I knew I would have to stroll through the park to make my way home. Unfortunately, the park was minus a certain suit. I was pathetic but I couldn't help myself, and over the next few days, I made more excuses to pass the watering hole at the exact time I had always seen him. Nothing. No appearance. Damn. Was he gone? Was he only in the city on business like me? Was he off on vacation? With his wife… and children? He must have a wife and children. Why would he come to the pond? *What was I saying?* I had no kids... no reason to come to the pond, but I loved the excitement... the noise... the suit. *At least I had work related distractions to keep me busy over the weekend,* I thought as I left the park.

When I got called into the theatre tonight, I was happy to go. I only went in occasionally, when performances were in full swing, since my work needed to be done while the theatre was empty. Also, I had such an amazing personal assistant, that she could handle any little task needed. Tonight, they were questioning parts of the set. There were some props that were not moving as they should. They wanted my input on lighting. They felt the contrast lighting was throwing off the dynamics. I had received some pretty strict instructs from Tamber about what he wanted in all aspects, including lighting, so I asked that they leave things as they were until I could contact him. He was one diva you did not want to mess with. Once I filled him in on the latest, I knew he would have suggestions and I wanted to keep the show in line with his visions. As I said, this was his gig; I was just the enforcer. Thankfully, Marco Zitti, the stage manager, was compliant.

Marco and Tamber were good friends and had worked together in various theatres around the country. This Boston production was their baby, and Marco knew better than to make big decisions without the diva's approval. I was always happy to work for or with either one of these amazing talents. I met Marco a couple years ago through Tamber and we became fast friends and, on a whim, we tossed in a few benefits that were very satisfying from time to time. Traveling could get lonely. Finding comfort in a warm body could be a welcomed treat. It didn't hurt that Marco was a tall, dark, gorgeous, Italian man with a very fit body.

After the performance wrapped for the evening, Marco asked me if I wanted to grab a drink or something. I knew what the something was and my raging hormones said, "What the hell?" First off, we popped next door to Abby Lane for an appetizer and a few cocktails served by an island tart who informed Marco her name was Kimee while she shoved her double-Ds in his face. That dark-skinned beauty had him going, and I was surprised he didn't push me out the door or ignore me totally. My best guess was that he knew I was a sure bet and less of a hot mess.

Back at my hotel room, we discarded our clothes and moved into action. There was no reason for foreplay. We had used each other enough over the years. We were always upfront and knew what this was all about. Both of us had needs. Only, this time, it wasn't doing it for me. My mind was back in the park with Mr. Suit. I was thinking about where he might have gone. A better question might be, who was he? Was he a dad in the park?

"Hey, Sofa, do you think you could put in a little more effort while I fuck you… maybe moan a little… a guy's ego can only handle so much rejection," Marco said looking down at me with a pouty look on his face, calling me by his favorite pet name for me, "Sofa."

"Sorry, Marco," I replied, pushing on his firm chest to move out from beneath him. Rolling off of me, we faced each other.

"Really? You're not going to let me, at least, finish?" He laughed as I pointed to his semi-limpness. "Shit!"

"I think we've run our course." Laughing, I got up, pulled on a robe, and returned, tossing a menu on the bed. "This arrangement has worked great . . . until now."

"Room service?" he asked as he reluctantly climbed off the bed and pulled on his clothes. "Who is he?"

"I don't know. Probably married. I see him at the Frog Pond. Probably has kids... one of the many splashing in the pond..." I picked up the phone receiver and ordered some highly caloric snacks for us to appease our frustrations while I confessed my semi-stalking behavior.

"Have you seen a wife and brats?"

"No... not that I know of..."

"Maybe he doesn't have any. You go to that place all the time and you're empty handed."

"He's a man. Besides he's too gorgeous to not be taken."

"Sofa, you are, too! Check it out next week, and maybe you should sit a little closer. I've never known you to be shy. You always go after what you want. If you want him, you may have to make the move. What's the worst thing that can happen? Some crazy, possessive wife pulls you away from him." Kissing me on the forehead,

Marco moved to the edge of the bed and slipped on his loafers. "I've gotta go. It's still early enough for me to take care of these blue balls." He always knew what to say to get me to laugh. "Come lock the door after me." I got up and followed him to the door.

"See you at the theatre tomorrow after I hear from Tamber. Sorry again about tonight."

With another kiss to the forehead, Marco started walking to the hotel door. "Don't worry about me, either my hand or that nice exotic bimbette will make it all better. Ciao." I was definitely not worried about him. Women were always falling at his feet. I was sure he would have no problem getting Kimee to spread her lush thighs for him.

Tossing my robe aside, I climbed back into welcomed empty bed. Well, maybe that wasn't exactly true. I would welcome a certain business man into my bed. Hmmm… I hoped Marco was right and maybe the suit was just like me; drawn to the fun, frenzied atmosphere at the watering hole. I could swear he looked at me with longing… *no, that was just wishful thinking on my part.* However, I did long for him, nestled between my thighs that were now moist and throbbing. Damn. Why didn't I put a little more effort into fucking Marco? I could've imagined Mr. Suit as he plunged into me. Sighing, I reached for my handy electric gadget and thought of my park man as I pleasured myself.

Chapter Three

SUNNY, WITH A chance of rain, was the forecast the weatherman announced as I shut off the TV and headed next door to the theatre. I needed to put Tamber's list into action and snap pictures and videos of the various goings on behind the scenes. Then I ironed out costume problems with the seamstress along with my ever-faithful personal assistant Lila. Good thing because Marco was a no-show; he was probably buried inside of the island temptress. Once we were done, I walked over to one of my favorite sandwich shops on Charles Street. They had amazing fresh baked bread and yummy homemade soups. I sat on a barstool by the window, eating a chicken tarragon sandwich, watching people stroll by with umbrellas at the ready. The sun was still peeking from behind clouds, so I hoped I would make it home before the rain poured down; I was without an umbrella.

On my way home, I thought maybe I should cut through the park. Yes, pass the Frog Pond. I smiled thinking perhaps he had returned and increased my pace. As I neared the watering hole, walking down a path off of Beacon Street, my heart started thudding when I saw a man on his bench. A gorgeous, dark-haired man in faded denims, a black fitted t-shirt, and a pair of loafers. I had never seen him casual. This was a first and I silently prayed, "Please don't let him have a wife," as I sat a few benches away from him; closer than usual. He was focusing on his phone screen and had not looked my way.

Not wanting to look out of place or a stalker, I pulled out my reader and attempted to read. It was no use, I understood nothing I read as I casually looked his way from time to time. I wasn't sure if he saw me or not. Little by little, dark clouds started rolling in. Then the sky lit up and thunder boomed. *Shit!* Time to go! Just *my* luck! Craziness started; kids and parents began running for shelter under the trees. I packed up my reader and joined everyone else and I noticed that Mr. Suit was gone.

Darting from tree to tree, I attempted to make my way to the nearest coffee shop without getting struck by lightning. Ducking my head, I ran firmly into a wall... a wall of rock hard man and I felt myself falling before two hands reached out and caught me. The strong hands kept me from plummeting to the ground but they were unable to keep me from hitting my head on the tree trunk. A loopy feeling came over me, causing me to sway and stagger forward until I was lifted up into muscular arms. Looking up into the lavender eyes of my rescuer, Mr. Suit, I gasped and slipped in and out of blackness, hearing words about a doctor friend. Then nothing.

Opening my eyes, I looked around an unfamiliar room with high ornate ceilings and exquisite moulding on the walls. I was in a large, foreign bed. Across the room, I saw handsome, Mr. Suit, seated in a chair, gazing at me. *What the fuck?* How did I get here? Then I remembered he scooped me up. Was I in his home?

"You're awake," he said as he stood and approached me. "How do you feel?" He sat on the edge of the bed; just out of reach.

Sitting up slowly, I glanced down and saw I was no longer in my clothes but in a silk robe that smelled musky and wonderful. "You undressed me?"

I sensed he was nervous by the way he began to rub the light stubble along his chin line. "You were soaking wet... I couldn't leave you like that. I closed my eyes while I did it..." I raised an eyebrow in his direction. He smiled and added, "I washed your clothing..."

"Thank you." I quietly looked at him, listening, as he began to explain more.

"I had my friend examine you... he's a doctor," he clarified immediately. "He said you couldn't be left alone. I've been sitting here since he left." Reaching his hand out, he slowly motioned to the back of my head. "You have a nasty bump on the back of your head."

I lifted my hand and felt the lump. "Ouch!"

"Your clothes should be dry soon. I can get you home..."

Not thinking about what I was saying, I blurted out, "I have no one to watch me."

I swear I saw a glimmer of light flash in his sexy eyes. "Oh."

Then coming to my senses, I realized I sounded pathetic. "No worry. I will be fine on my own."

"No." His voice was stern. "You can stay with me. I will watch you."

"That's not necessary. You don't even know me."

"Then I guess this is a good time to introduce ourselves because I insist you stay." Putting his hand in mine, he said, "I'm Drake Blaxton. And you are?"

Trying to control the sensations jolting through my body as he continued to hold my hand, I managed to utter my name. "Sofie James." He smiled.

"Nice to meet you, Sofie. Are you hungry? You've been resting for a few hours. I ordered some food to be delivered. I can bring it to you or you can come downstairs to eat."

I knew he said something about food but I couldn't get past those eyes. Lavender eyes. "You have unusual eyes. Only one other time have I ever seen eyes that color; an upset woman in the park the other day. Do you have a sister?"

"Not that I know about," he said, letting go of my hand and standing. "Blaxton men have been known to stray." Backing up he gave me room to climb out of bed and then held out his hand to me. "Come, let's get you some food."

I pulled back the comforter, took his hand, and he pulled me up. Touching him and breathing was a difficult task. I needed to pull myself together. "Will your wife mind that I'm in your guest room?" He laughed softly at my question.

"I have no wife... and you are in my bed." One helluva sexy grin followed his words and my heart beat rapidly. I wondered if it would be out of line if I pulled him onto the bed rather than let him lead me away. What would he do if I stood and dropped the silk robe he had tied around me? He had already seen me nude. Did he like what he saw? I smiled to myself. I hoped he did. I loved the way his one hand held my arm and the other was splayed on my low back as he helped me walk down the open staircase lit by a beautiful wall sconces and a chandelier hanging down the middle for the ceiling high above. His touch warmed me to the core.

At the bottom of the staircase, we reached the foyer and turned right to walk down a wide hallway, passing a parlor, a formal, very elegant dining room, and into a modern wood and stainless steel decorated kitchen. "Your home is spectacular. It reminds me of the Prescott townhouse . . . minus all the Victorian decor."

"My house is down the way from the townhouse, and you're right; it does have similarities. Would you like to sit in the dining room or here in the kitchen?"

"The kitchen is good." As long as I could be near him, it really didn't matter.

"Good," he said, releasing his hold on me and I instantly missed the closeness. "Have a seat." I climbed on to one of the high stools placed around the center island and watched him intently. God, he was so gorgeous. "I ordered soup and bread from one of my favorite places; Panificio Bistro and Bakery." He removed soup containers and poured the semi-warm liquid into a pot on the stovetop, then popped the slender bread loaf into the oven. "Shouldn't take long to crust up the baguette." He moved back to the paper sacks on the granite countertops. "I got us a little sweet treat." He smiled as he removed a pastry box and dangled it by the string that held it closed.

"Oh… I love that place. I went there earlier. I had a sandwich. I wanted soup but they were running late and apologized."

"Well, perfect. Now you will get to taste their soup of the day."

Once everything was heated, he served up two bowls and the wonderfully crisped bread with creamy, unsalted butter. We sipped the delicious, bacon potato cheese soup, facing each other. I was amazed I was able to eat while he continuously gazed into my eyes. "You said you were alone. Alone in the city? Or alone?"

"Alone," I said softly and waited for his response before I dared to take another bite.

"Good," was all he said. We finished our meal in silence. Once our bowls were empty, he cleaned up the kitchen. I tried to help, but he ordered me to stay put. I sat still and enjoyed the view. When everything was spic and span, he told me he was going to check on my clothes. Upon his return, he handed me folded clothing.

"Thank you," I said looking around, "do you have a powder room downstairs?"

"Yes, let me show you."

Inside the bathroom, I untied his robe. It smelt so manly and felt so good against my bare skin; I would've rather kept it on. Looking in the mirror, I blushed thinking of him seeing me nude and a chill ran intimately down my spine. Dressed, minus shoes, I exited the bathroom, with his robe draped over my arm, and returned to the kitchen, but he was not there. I looked in dining room; empty as well. When I stopped at the entrance to the parlor, I saw him sitting on a sofa.

Stepping into the room, I placed his robe on the back of a chair and joined him on a low profile, modern, tweed couch. Taking the glass, he posed in my direction. I settled back and turned to face the glorious man. *Please don't let this be a dream.* "Thank you for helping me."

"It was my pleasure. Not that you were hurt but that I have your attention. That I finally have you in my home."

"Oh?" I questioned, looking at him, waiting for him continue. I wanted to tell him I was thrilled to be close to him, too. That I longed for him for the last few weeks, but I stayed quiet. I would let him speak first. Besides, I didn't wish to make a fool of myself.

"I've been going to the park almost daily since I saw you a few weeks ago, except for weekends. Then last week, I had to fly to Hong Kong on business. I missed you. I was happy to see you reading on a bench in the park today, when I looked up after finishing my business call. I've been wondering if you were married." I shook my head no. "If you were in the park with your children?" I shook my head again. "I haven't been able to get you out of my head. I've been feeling like such a stalker."

I couldn't let him confess without confessing myself. "You are not the only one. I've been making an effort to get to the park about the same time every day that you usually appear."

"Some days I would watch you from afar before going to my usual spot. I wanted to see if anyone would approach you. And then it happened. I was watching you biting on the end of your pen and I wish that..." He stopped with a devilish grin painted across his handsome face.

"You wished what?" I could imagine what he meant but I wanted to hear it. I wanted to hear he wanted me. He desired me as I desired him.

"Let's just say that my lustful fantasy ended when two small children approached you. I had my answer; you belonged to someone else. Defeated, I watched the joy on your face as they appeared to tell you tales and your laughter struck me deep. It delighted me. I wished the two rug-rats were mine... ours... that I was coming to meet you in the park. Sadly, knowing they weren't mine, I looked one more time in your direction before I trudged home. Head down, I turned away and walked to this big empty townhouse that begs for a family to occupy it. Every time I walk through the front doors I feel like it groans, 'only you'. I commiserated with the house. I questioned why it was not filled with a wife and children. Why was there no one to greet me? I was miserable all weekend long. I drank a lot of scotch and slipped into a cold, empty, lonely bed every night and thought of you. God, I sound pathetic." He swallowed a gulp of wine.

"Not at all. I had similar thoughts about you. I was jealous when I saw you speaking with a woman and a child one day. I was certain you were married. I was thankful that no one approached you today. I wanted to sit on a bench closer to you to see if you would speak to me but I didn't know if you were waiting to meet a wife, or if one of the giggling, laughing, splashing kids belonged to you. You seemed so out of place at the pond, in your suit, unless... unless you were there for your family."

"I imagine a business suit in the summer at the pond did look a bit out of place. I actually love stopping by the pond; it brings back great memories. As a kid, I played for hours at the Frog Pond, day after day in the summer and ice skated on it during the winter. I hadn't really sat down at the pond in a long while for any length of time. Yes, I've strolled by now and again between my office and home. Then one day, I saw a vision of loveliness that took my breath away. I had to see you again. Every time I saw you, I wanted you..."

I cut him off. I couldn't take anymore. "I wanted you, too." Those four words were all it took for me to find myself in his warm embrace with his mouth crushing mine. I gasped as his teeth sunk into my bottom lip. He liked to bite, did he? We were going to get along perfectly. I smiled against his lips before biting him back then licked his assaulted lip and sucked it in between mine. I heard various animalistic groans as our tongues vigorously attacked each other.

"Oh fuck. Why did I ever give you your clothes back?"

I laughed. "So you liked what you saw earlier?"

"I don't remember," he said between nibbles. "It's been too long. Refresh my memory."

"Why don't you undress me? Apparently, you're an expert and I never got to watch before…" The last word barely left my lips, with a few swift moves, I found myself being carried out of the parlor and into the foyer.

"Where are we going?"

He moved to the wooden staircase and began to climb. "Where I unclothed you last time. Only this time, I won't be gentle and you won't be doing any resting until I've had my fill." He groaned and stopped. "God you're beautiful." Then he dipped his head and bit my lip, causing me to moan. While he continued his ascent, I bit and licked his neck. "Oh fuck. We are going to be so fucking good together."

In his room, settled on my feet, only steps away from the bed, he removed every article of clothing from his body. I thoroughly enjoyed every hard inch he revealed. Mmmm... his chest, his abs, his v-cut over his hips and *holy shit*, the most delicious cock I had ever seen. It was thick and huge, begging to have my teeth scrape along it before sucking it deep into my throat. I licked my lips and heard a sexy chuckle. "You like what you see?"

"Yes, but I'd much rather feel it..." I hesitated but I had waited long enough; no reason to be shy now. "I want you inside of me." I've never had clothes leave my body so fast in my life. Maybe torn from my body may be a better description.

Pushed back onto the bed, I heard the tear of foil before I felt complete and utter fullness as he sunk deep into my body. I wrapped my legs over his and met him thrust for thrust. Our bodies were aligned perfectly. Feverishly biting at each other's necks, we panted and moaned. Pushing harder and harder, I cried out his name along with "*yes*" in a chanting fashion. He connected to the right spot... oh... oh so perfectly over and over and over. Never had I ever reached such an earth-shattering climax through penetration alone. I knew I had hit my head hard early and I prayed once again, "please don't let this be a dream."

Chapter Four

WOW. WAS THIS really happening? Was I really lying in bed next up the Frog Pond suit man? Yes, yes I was. His glorious body was warm and hard; it matched mine with such perfection. We fit like a glove. He made me feel so alive. So on fire. I was definitely not a virgin but sex with him awakened emotions… feelings… senses. What had he done to me? What had he not done to me? Somehow I felt like he'd turned my world upside down. I felt like things had changed in me. That I would never be the same. Wow. What was up with me? Why was I having all of these crazy ideas about a stranger? A beautiful stranger… but still a stranger.

Just yesterday, this stranger brought me to his bedroom, stripped me, and then gave me great pleasure all night long. Well… there was the between time that he cared for me and fed me, but my mind couldn't get passed the passion I felt for this man. The man I was watching as he slept. His lightly stubbled, chiseled face was beautiful and I had the urge to tug my fingers through his dark hair. His long black, full, thick eyelashes rested on his cheek bones, concealing those incredible eyes. Yum… his full lips made fuller by my teeth and lips. I felt the need to sink my teeth into every inch of his skin. I could eat him up. I moaned quietly, thinking of how many times we had brought each to such incredible screaming orgasms.

Turning away from the hotness, I saw a few lavender panes mixed with clear glass in two large, curved, multi-paned windows. Pulling back the covers, I padded across the cool, wood-planked flooring to get a closer look. Standing right in front of the window, I saw The Commons across the street and a hint of the Frog Pond through the trees. Hmmm... he was never far from the famous watering hole. I found that interesting as I stood naked gazing out, then back to him. I was with him... the suited man... the gorgeous man... Drake... Drake...

"If you're going to say my name, I'd prefer that you were under me."

Turning, I saw a hard body completely visible. Yes, he was smiling slyly as he exposed himself. Oh that body... those muscles... that hardness... I rushed back to the bed and pressed into him as our mouths locked and our tongues and teeth attacked. I was so ready to have him buried deep inside of me again. I could spend forever connected with him.

"Mmmm... Sofie, darling, as much I would like to take you again, I think your body needs a break. You have to be sore. I know I was rough with you. I'm not apologizing though. I will do it again . . . and again to you, but..."

Squirming and wiggling into him, I wanted him. I

didn't care that I was sore; I was wet, throbbing, and feeling so empty. "I am deliciously sore."

"You need a break." I felt his grip on me loosen.

"Absolutely not." I pouted and moved into him. "I can take all that you can give."

It was no use; he disentangled from my clutches, laughing. "I'm going to give you breakfast."

I smiled, thinking he had changed his mind. "Yum... what did you have in mind?" I asked as I snuggled a little closer to his retreating body and nibbled his neck. He tasted so good.

"Coffee. Toast. Bacon. Juice. Fruit."

"Awww..." I tried the sad eye look but he just laughed and planted another mind blowing kiss on my mouth before he pulled away, stood up, and extended his hand.

"Come... We can have a shower first." Tugging me up, I crawled up his body, wrapped my legs around his waist, and sunk my teeth into his neck. I heard him groan and I knew he would give in to me as he walked us into a large tiled shower stall. I hoped with my little coaxing moves, I would have him sliding me up and down the wall while I was impaled on his glorious cock. I may not be able to walk to breakfast, but I would be deliciously sated.

Emerging from the shower smiling, wearing an enormous smile, we dressed, then made our way out onto the bustling street, and hailed a cab. "I want to take you to my favorite place for breakfast and then I'm going to give you a special tour of Beacon Hill."

"Sounds great but I would really love some fresh clothes first. After breakfast, we can stop by my hotel, yes?"

"Better idea. We can shop right after breakfast. We'll be surrounded by retail... here we are." Yes. Here we were, pulled up in front of my beloved morning spot. I shook my head in disbelief. "What's wrong, Sofie?"

"Nothing." I smiled. "Nothing at all."

Walking through the glass front door, Sherry spotted us immediately and made her way over. "Well look at this; Lavender Britches and Honeybee."

We grinned at each other and Drake spoke up. "Another place we have in common?"

"Looks like it," I answered as we walked to my usual spot by the window. "Do you have a favorite table?"

Taking a seat, he smiled. "You're sitting at it."

"Mine, too. Good thing we never frequented the cafe at the same time. We would've had to flip for the table." I laughed.

"I would've asked you to join me." He smiled, making his eyes twinkle, and I melted on the spot.

Sherry cut in on our conversation. "There was no way that would've ever happened. You two are creatures of habit. She only comes here on weekdays and you only come in on weekends."

"She's right. My weekends are usually reserved for sleeping in. You've broken my habit." I was happy he interrupted my schedule, although, we could've stayed in his bed.

"The usual for both of you? Or… since you're breaking your routines, would you like to hear the breakfast… or lunch specials?" We both laughed, shaking our heads. I guess we really were as she said, "creatures of habit", as we both stated our usual breakfasts. Sherry promptly stepped away, without handing us menus, and returned with our coffees just how we liked them.

"I love this place. I've been coming here for a few weeks now. Love seeing Sherry and hearing the different names she gives certain customers. How long have you been coming here, Lavender Britches?" I grinned.

Straight faced he looked at me. "Well, Honeybee…" I laughed, causing him to lose his composure before he could continue. "I've been coming here as long as Sherry has worked here. I followed her from her last two restaurants. She's like family."

"Aah. A true regular," I said as our food arrived.

"Yes, dahling, I've known him since he was in toddler britches and I was in hot pants and go-go boots, working in a retro diner," Sherry informed me as she placed my special veggie and cheese, one-egg omelette in front of me and eggs Benedict before Drake. He must've been adorable as a little tyke, I thought, smiling to myself and she confirmed my assumption. "He was cute as a button… still is…" She nudged him. "Enjoy your breakfast… hollah if you need something." Patting my shoulder, she strode off to the next table to entertain her other customers.

Finished eating, we said our goodbyes but not without Drake planting a kiss on Sherry's cheek first. He then guided me in and out of shops along Newbury Street. I tried to make a purchase in the first shop, however, I was reprimanded then informed that since shopping was his idea, his credit card would be used. Also, as the purchaser of my new wardrobe, he had two firm requests. One: I had to model everything—lingerie included. Secondly, pants nor shorts were allowed. Hmmm... he had interesting demands. I could only imagine his reasoning and it sent chills up and down my spine thinking about them. By the end of our spree, we both carried several designer store bags filled with lingerie, summer dresses, skirts, tops, and sandals (both high heeled and flat).

After hailing us a cab to his townhouse, Drake allowed me just enough time to change into a red sundress and bronze-bejeweled, flat sandals before we flew out the front door to roam the many narrow cobblestone streets of Beacon Hill. Walking along the brick sidewalks lined with flowering pear trees, he pointed out the various architectural elements of Greek Revival, Victorian, and Colonial that, combined, made up the Federal style of brick row houses. My favorites were the red brick facades with white wood-trimmed, multi-paned glass window, including some purple panes, black shutters, and window boxes with cascading flowers, and framed white wood moulding around black lacquered doors with ornate brass door knockers.

Loved all the greenery; large potted trees with flowers, and the secret gardens hidden behind pretty decorative black iron fencing and gates. It was charming the way bright green moss grew on cobblestones in shady areas. Viewing a distant fountain in a private garden behind one of the ornate fences, I sighed and Drake, insisting we get a closer look, reached over and unlatched the gate.

"We can't go in there." I hesitated.

"It's not locked. I don't see a 'no trespassing' sign. Do you?" I shook my head and he pulled me through the gate and down a long, narrow alleyway between two brick buildings that lead to brownstone with a red lacquer door. Dropping my hand, he walked right up to the door and knocked. When no one answered, he grasped my hand and led me to one of the benches in the private garden. The space was gorgeous; green grass, planters filled with fruit trees, fragrant flowers, and white lace trellises with climbing lavender clematis vines which screened in the lush, private garden.

"We shouldn't be here," I said as he slipped off my sandals, propped my feet in his lap, and began to rub them tenderly. My shoe selection may have been wrong but they sure looked good. Mmmm... I closed my eyes and let him sooth my aching feet but promptly opened them as his hand slid up my leg, under my dress, and ripped off my panties. Covering his hand, I attempted to stop his approach, but intense, darkened lavender eyes burnt into my skin, stilling my moaned complaints. I opened my legs, giving his skillful fingers full access. I gasped as my first orgasm of the afternoon rushed over me and made me long for more.

More is exactly what I got as Drake grasped my hips and pulled me up onto to his lap so I was straddling him. I was about to protest as my dress was moved up around my waist when suddenly, his mouth captured mine and I forgot all about where we were. I gave in to his desires. Smiling, he slid the straps of my dress off my shoulders, exposing my ample breasts and my nipples instantly pebbled; begging for his attention. "Mmmm…" I moaned as he caressed and kneaded, then alternating between them with his lips, tongue, and his teeth. I grounded into him until yet another orgasm roared from my body.

"I need to catch up," I heard him groan as he reached between my legs, freed himself, and filled me. "Ride me, Sofie." I heard and did exactly as I was instructed. Sliding up and down his delicious hardness, panting and moaning, I felt the rise of yet another beautiful climax. Only this time, I was not alone in my pleasure. Devouring my mouth with his, he drown out our sounds and thrust faster and harder until the waves finally subsided. Breathlessly, I slumped against his firm chest and thanked him.

"Mmmm… Now that you've drained me of all energy in the most delightful way, perhaps you would like to buy me dinner and refuel me."

My remark gained me a hardy laugh and a suggestion. "How does traditional French gourmet cuisine sound?"

"Divine. Lead the way." Clothes straightened, we left the private garden, exited through the iron gate, and made our way to The Hungry I restaurant, a converted and restored 1840 brownstone on Charles Street.

Greeting us, the maître'd suggested we sit in their secret garden dining and walked us through the restaurant; showing us the vine-covered patio. It was delightful with its grey, slatted walls, bright-green framed windows that were adorned by planted window boxes, and dark-grey painted brick that transitioned into exposed brick above the vines. There were several draped, small bistro tables with wrought iron chairs complimented by striped pillow cushions. I found the space charming, but we opted for inside. Redirected inside, we were shown three cozy, intimate dining rooms, featuring the continuation of exposed brick walls embellished with oil paintings, fireplaces, beautiful antiques, and tables dressed with white linens. The soft glow from candlelight dining added to the ambiance of the rooms. We settled for side by side seating on upholstered banquettes with embroidered decorative pillows. Drake insisted that he be able to touch me at all times as we dined. Yum. I understood why he said the restaurant was billed as the most romantic restaurant in Boston.

Looking over the deliciously tempting menu, we decided to share everything in courses. We started with two dirty martinis and appetizers; egg-battered shrimp with a Ginger-Sherry dipping sauce and Frog leg

Provencal. Both were fabulous. Course two was a salad of feta and apricot crisps on a bed of spinach leaves. When it came to the main course, we selected two amazing entrees because we couldn't decide on just one: loin of Lamb Latrec and breast of Duck L'Orange. For dessert we settled on one of their most famous sweet treats, a Raspberry Blackberry Linzer tarte, to savour at home.

Strolling home hand-in-hand, Drake resumed his architectural lesson, continuing on as we arrived at and toured his townhouse. So far, I had only seen the first floor parlour, dining room, powder room, and kitchen. Tonight I was shown the laundry room and back staircase with access to all floors that were to be used by staff and children in decades of the past. At one time, the fourth floor housed servants and featured a children's playroom. Back in the day, children were not allowed to use the front stairs except on special occasions. "I cannot imagine," Drake remarked after giving me the lowdown about the fourth floor. "I want this house filled with screaming children, sliding down the front staircase bannisters."

I laughed and shook my head as we walked up the front stairs. "I think you might want to rethink that statement. Sliding down these railing could be dangerous and I don't know about screaming children. Laughing, lovable, happy, giggling children sound better."

Reaching the second floor, he quickly showed me two more bedrooms with an adjoining bathroom between them. I didn't need to be shown the master suite as I was quite familiar with it, so we moved up to the next floor. On the third floor, there was an office/library that looked out to The Commons. The room had a floor to ceiling bookcase filled with many hardbound books along one wall and a sliding ladder. A vintage, hand-carved mahogany wood desk, which once belonged to his great-grandfather, sat in front of the window. The reading space was decorated with modern furnishings: a sofa, a coffee table, and two club chairs arranged on a large antique area rug. Leaving the room, Drake quickly showed me a nicely decorated guest bedroom with an en suite bathroom. We then headed to the back of the house, finding a game room complete with a bar and billiard table before continuing out two sliding doors to his deck.

When I walked out on to the deck, I notice the reproduction sliding patio doors had purple glass similar to the old panes in the original house windows. Touching them, I turned to Drake and began to ask but he answered before a word escaped my lips. "Yes, I obtained an old window through a local auction house and had them installed."

Moving me away from the doors, we settled on a wide, padded lounge chair large enough for two. "They match your eyes."

Ignoring my statement about his eyes, he unstrapped and removed my sandals then asked, "You know about the lavender glass?"

"I heard it was an error." Those were the only words

I managed to say as he rid me of my dress.

He went on to explain the history behind the glass while stroking my bare skin. "Yes. Too much manganese oxide was used while the panes were manufactured. This caused the glass to turn a lavender shade, giving off, what they call, an *Amethyst Glow*. I love this part of my job as an architect; learning design and decor concepts and how historical elements come into play."

Finishing his glass lesson, he removed his own clothing, exposing his hard body. I moaned at the sight and he rubbed up against me. "Mmmm... This is the perfect city for an architect. It fascinates me. It's gotta be a wet dream for your profession."

"Ha! That's a first. I don't believe I've ever heard Beantown architecture referred to in such a sexual way. Hmmm... something to think about. Occasionally, I write articles for a few design magazines. That idea could make for interesting research."

"You could start with your own building. It's mouthwatering. The ornate beams and mouldings send chills down my spine... and the way the..."

I was cut short when a sexy, warm, lush mouth covered mine and then I heard words whispered softly against my lips, "You can't fuck my townhouse but you can fuck me," before he silenced all conversation for good.

Chapter Five

A WAKENED BY A kiss. I was living a fairytale. A little over a week had passed and every morning I was provided a goodbye kiss or two from the owner of the warm, cozy bed I inhabited in a townhouse on Beacon Street. This morning was no different except that I received a lunch offer I could not refuse. "Meet me for lunch at my office. We'll have a picnic looking out over the *Emerald Necklace.*" I mumbled my answer then felt the covers being pulled back, and a set of teeth sunk into my backside. I moaned and waited for more but instead, I was re-covered. "The view is spectacular."

"Are you speaking of my body or the city?" I giggled and rolled on to my back, exposing my breasts to two beautiful, ogling, lavender eyes.

"You don't play fair, Sofie." *My* fully suited handsome man attacked my breasts with his tongue, teeth and lips; with my fingers in his hair, I held on tight. Unfortunately, he was only giving me a sampling of his fabulous techniques and broke free from my grasp. I pouted, groaning my displeasure. He laughed and assured me there would definitely be a lot more, later. "I have a meeting this morning or I would fuck you properly. Come to lunch and I will give you what you want."

I accepted defeat and pulled the covers up, concealing my lonely nipples. "Okay," I huffed then added, "I suppose I'm to bring the food?"

One more delicious kiss was granted to me. "All I need is you for lunch; spread out naked on my desk."

I laughed as he strolled away. I called out to him. "I will bring food as well!"

When *my* gorgeous man was no longer in view, I rolled over and moved to Drake's side of the bed. Clutching his pillow, I burrowed my nose to take in his scent and fell back to sleep until my cellphone started ringing. Ring! Quiet. Ring! Quiet. Ring! *Damn!* I knew that "Hey There Delilah" ringtone; it had to be important.

"Good morning, Lila." Apparently it wasn't a good morning for her and she let me know about all the drama that unfolded. An actor had a hissy fit the night before and broke several stage props. My assistant had to gather them all up and take inventory. Ugh! She asked where she could find similar items. I knew of thrift/antique stores in the area, and let her know I would go shopping if she would text me the items along with snapshots of said broken pieces. Then I dragged myself out of bed, showered and headed with a list over to Charles Street. I actually loved to visit these shops—they had amazing deals; bring your own paper sack and fill them for $10 to $30 per bag. There would be no problem finding theatre props or even a few fun treasures for myself and, of course, something for Lila. Finished, I made my way to the theatre with two overflowing bags.

Going through the various finds, we threw out all of the old stuff, salvaged a few, and arranged the new pieces with each scene setting. Once we were all organized, I let Marco know that if his actor broke another item I would be breaking his fucking fingers. He just laughed at me and tenderly rubbed my shoulders before turning me loose to answer my buzzing phone. Aah! A naughty text from Drake; a reminder that I needed to get to his office with his lunch.

Time to have a little fun with him. "Not sure I can make it."

"Not an option. I have an erected building that needs your full attention. Every inch. Every detail needs to be examined. I have the perfect avenue in mind for it to rest in."

"Hmmm… on one condition."

"Name it."

"You must be completely nude when I arrive."

"Done. Make sure you're here on time—12:30 sharp!"

Looking at the time on my phone, I quickly said my goodbyes, insured that Lila could handle things for the rest of the day, and then left the theatre. Rushing next door to my hotel suite, I freshened up: threw on a turquoise halter dress, high heeled silver sandals, silver hoop earrings, a silver cuff bracelet around bicep, and pulled my hair up in to a high ponytail. Yes, no undergarments.

Ready to go, I went down to the lobby and waited as my doorman hailed a cab for me. I headed for one of my favorite gourmet, Italian delicatessens in the North End, complete with a charming and handsome deli-man. As I walked in through the front glass door of the narrow store, incredibly delish smells enveloped me and my stomach began to growl. I was starving and suddenly wanted everything the deli had to offer. However, I did refuse samples; I knew I would be full by the time I left the shop if I tried it all. Besides, I knew it would all be heavenly. Mouthwatering delights called to me behind glass cases; a wide variety of marinated items such as cheese, homemade pasta, and potato salads. Yum. I selected a pint of sun-dried tomato and feta pasta salad, a quarter of garlic marinated mushrooms, three different types of olives, sliced meats (prosciutto, pepperoni, salami, and capocollo), cheeses (manchego, sharp provolone), and a loaf of crusty, Italian bread. To accompany our feast, I added some Italian cookies, a bottle of Acqua Panna sparkling water and a bottle Sangiovese wine.

While the nice deli-man packed everything into a lovely wicker basket filled with assortment of picnic accessories, I plucked a bag of sugarcoated pastel almonds, a favorite of mine. Now, I was set for today's lunch.

Situated in the backseat of the taxi again; the driver

transported me across town to the Prudential Center. Entering the building, I struggled my way passed several shops and through a crowd of shoppers with my rather heavy picnic basket. I really hadn't thought this through, but I was determined to get the basket up to the 38th floor unassisted. Riding up the elevator, I thought back to the last time I was in this building to visit the Skywalk Observatory on the 50th floor. I was taking clients to see the amazing view of Boston before having cocktails and appetizers at the Top of the Hub restaurant and lounge on the 52nd floor. This visit would be far more inti-mate... and exciting.

Stepping off of the elevator, I entered a large, open reception area. The waiting section in the space had highly polished, concrete floors, decorated with black leather and chrome Le Corbusier chairs, arranged around a thick, grey-green sea-glass oval table, topped with a metal framed miniature building. I walked up to the reception desk, gave my name, informing her that I had a meeting with Mr. Blaxton. The woman at the desk was very cordial and gave me directions to his office; pointing the way with a smile of her face.

Proceeding to my sexy lunch destination, I walked past several beechnut wood panels, framed with stainless steel down along one wall. Multiple metal pedestals housed architectural models under glass boxes in front of each panel. The structures were all different and quite impressive. I wondered how many had Drake created as I arrived in front of a desk, sitting outside a closed door, marked with the words "Drake Blaxton." I was greeted with a smile by a middle-aged secretary who immediately spoke into a headset.

"Mr. Blaxton, your lunch has arrived… Yes, sir. I'll be back at two o'clock." Then to me, she said, "Go right in. Enjoy your lunch," as she grabbed her purse, stood, and walked away.

I knocked before strolling in to a glorious sight. I smiled.

"As you see…" He stretched out his bare muscular arms. "I can be very obedient."

"Mmmm… your office has an amazing view…" I settled the picnic basket on a low wood table in front of a black leather diamond tufted sofa, admired the framed architectural sketches mounted on the walls of his office, and then walked to the windows. He was right, part of the *Emerald Necklace of Boston* was visible looking out his floor to ceiling windows; the tree-lined streets formed a necklace chain, and The Commons made up the emerald pendant. "Spectacular," I said as I turned away from the window to see him swivel his chair in my direction. There he sat behind his massive desk. He had done as I had requested. My eyes were instantly drawn to his big, muscular legs and the beautiful erection proudly on display for me.

Standing before him I reached behind my neck, and untied my dress. Letting it fall to the floor, "ooh… fuck me," escaped from Drake's two biteable lips.

I purred, "I plan on it." Seeing him start to move, I

raised my hand. "Stay put." I slowly moved to his chair, climbed up, straddled his legs and lowered myself onto him in one swift move. Grabbing my ponytail firmly in the middle, he twisted my hair around his hand, pulled me in close, and attacked my mouth; biting and licking and plundering. I rode him briefly, moaning into his mouth then I broke away, rose up, and removed my body from his. Backing up, biting my lip, I stood, looking at him.

"Don't tease me," he groaned and I silently sunk to my knees before him. Lowering my mouth over his cock, I raked my teeth up and down his hard length.

"Oh, Sofie, that feels incredible." I knew he liked teeth and biting so I continued with my method and sucked him in deep. Tasting his pre-cum and my own juices mixed together was erotic and it spurred me on. I had never wanted to worship a man's body so much in my life. My nipples were rock hard and I was soaking wet; moisture dripped down my legs. I was teetered on the edge of my own climax; one touch and I would've burst. "You're killing me, Sofie… ooh baby… I'm going to come…" I felt him try to pull me up and I moved more vigorously, incorporating the squeeze of my hand around the base of his shaft. Relaxing his grasp, pushing his hips forward, he exploded in my mouth and I drank every drop, licking him clean. Looking up into Drake's darkened lavender eyes, he announced, "I'm starving," with a wicked grin before he reached for me.

"I brought lots of food."

Twirling my ponytail, he raised an eyebrow. "I need an appetizer."

"Oh… that I didn't bring."

"I see one right in front of me." Then before I could speak another word, I found myself spread wide open on his desk top, his mouth devouring me. I shamelessly grasped his hair and rode his face as he licked, sucked, and bit me. One orgasm rolled out after another and he kept them coming as he curled two fingers inside of me, rubbing a magical spot. Panting wildly, I wanted to scream but instead, I put my hand to my mouth and bit down hard on the pad below my thumb.

Delicious swipes of his tongue soothed me as my climaxes waned and then he licked and nipped his way up my body, making me treble and quake. *God, how I hoped he was going to fill me, I silently prayed.* I desperately needed him to ease my throbbing as he sucked each of my nipples in his mouth. Then he rewarded me; capturing my mouth and – plunging his solid length deep inside of me… filling me… rocking into me… grinding… rolling his hips… he was sending me straight to heavenly bliss. Thank God our mouths were connected as our climaxes collided; otherwise the entire building would know that lunch wasn't the only thing on Mr. Blaxton's agenda. Regaining our natural breathing, Drake helped me off of his desk and guided me to his sitting area.

"You brought a feast," he said as I revealed the contents of my picnic basket and began to place the treats on the table after I spread out the red and white checked tablecloth.

"I did go overboard. Not a good idea to shop for food while hungry."

Grabbing two seat cushions off of the couch, he placed them on the floor on either side of the wood table and we ate lunch sans clothing. "I wish this was a glass table."

"Why is that?" I asked coyly, knowing perfectly well what he meant and I felt a warm hand slip between my legs. "Mmmm… is it essential you see what you desire?"

Those words prompted him to grab his phone from the sofa, making a call to his secretary. He told her to take the rest of the day off and that he'd see her on Monday morning. Then he tossed the phone, hurdled the table, and made me come completely undone over and over. By the time we left Drake's office, the stars were out and everyone had gone home for the night.

Chapter Six

O VER THE WEEKEND, Drake and I participated in our usual routine: Saturday breakfast with Sherry, walking, talking, shopping, cooking… and of course a lot of mutual body appreciation time. Added to our usual shopping list, which was mainly consisted of fresh food and beverages, was to find a glass table, purchase it, and set up delivery for Monday morning. I was informed that I would be required to deliver lunch to the 38th floor on a regular basis. I was more than happy to oblige his said demand.

After searching through a variety of furniture shops, the perfect table was selected. A thick clear glass top, supported by four wooden legs that reminded us of bed posts. There was something so sexy about that table and it matched his office so precisely. It had a blend of modern meets old world style like his office with its modern furnishings and antique framed architectural drawings.

"The ornate elements on this table look like the frames in your office. Are they all your drawings… your projects?"

"Yes, they are all mine. Is that all you think of when

you see the table?" A smirk played on his gorgeous face, but I ignored his question.

"I noticed the largest and more prominent piece, over the sofa, was a theatre design interior and exterior. Exquisite details. I'd love to see it."

"Yes." He smiled proudly, puffing out his strong chest. "You are not the only theatrical one in this relationship…"

Relationship; that was the only words I heard as he continued speaking about the theatre design, I assumed. I would have to google it later or admit to the fact that I had zoned out. How could I think about anything but that *big* word; it hung out, above all other important nouns. It sent my mind reeling; imagine having a real relationship with him instead of what I called a vacation/business encounter. What we had was not real. It was fun, but could never work; he was East Coast and I was West Coast. We were both established in our careers. No. Sadly, this was only for a short time and nothing more than a fabulous way to pass it.

"Sofie… Sofie?" Two strong hands cupped my face, forcing me to look into lavender eyes. "Hey . . . what's with the sad look… and tears?" With his thumbs, he gently wiped the moisture from my cheeks. "Where did you go?"

Reaching up, I placed my hands over his wrists, leaned my forehead on his chest and lied, "I'm sorry. I don't know." I couldn't tell him the truth. I couldn't tell him that my heart would break when I departed. No, this needed to be a happy fling with no drama. Funny words for a person whose life was surrounded, literally, by drama daily. Different drama. Pulling away from Drake, I wiped my eyes and waved my hand, laughing. "Raging hormones... a girlee thing." Then I changed the subject and got him to take me for an ice cream at our infamous watering hole. Happy to fulfill my request, he never questioned me further and I was delighted the rest of the weekend. The next week was filled with sheer pleasure; indoors and out.

WORK AT THE theatre was smooth and uneventful, just the way I liked it. It enabled me to work on my production design sketches and have brunch with Marco at the end of the week. I hadn't seen much of him since he wasn't needed during the day and I hadn't been needed at night. It was nice to catch up on the latest gossip and chit chat about our new found friends in Boston.

"A bunch of us are going to Shakespeare in the Park; bring your park man and come along. He does exist, right? All of what you just told me is real? You're not just fantasizing about him while drooling from your frog bench?"

"Yes. I guess I never told you what happened, only that we're seeing each other."

"Helloooo!—I haven't seen you lately," he states, dramatically.

"Well… that's because I've been playing house with Drake and you've been playing limbo with your well-endowed, island honey."

Ignoring my island girl comment, he grilled me. "Oh. He has an actual name and a house?"

I beamed just thinking about him. "Yes. On Beacon Hill."

Slapping his hand on the table, he exclaimed, "Shit! I hate him already!"

Shaking my head, I laughed at him, then proceeded to tell him the details about the lightning, hitting my head, being carried to his home, and taken care of thoroughly. Minus the good details.

"Holy shit sounds like a fucking romance novel. You sure he's real? You didn't hit your head too hard and just imagining this shit?"

"It's real. We haven't spent a night apart since." I couldn't stop the smile that lit my face.

"Oh my God… Sofa's in love!" Damn, he was annoying singing *Drake and Sofa sitting in a tree…* loudly. I was not in love. I had never been in love ever in my life. *Imagine having my first love at thirty-one years old.* No, this was just lust. Wasn't it? Yes, it was. I shook my head as he continued, "I can see the answer in your eyes. That's it. Time to share him. I need to see if he's worthy. Invite him now; dessert and drinks at Finale and then Shakespeare in the Park."

"Oh, I've been dying to go there. I've passed it a bazillion times and drooled looking in the windows.

Yummy pastry!"

"Don't change the subject."

"Sounds like fun, but I don't know." Why was I hesitant? Maybe I just wanted to keep him all to myself.

"Sofa, text him now."

"Okay... okay... I'll see if he's up for it." Digging my phone out of my new leopard Michael Kor handbag, I typed. "How do you feel about dessert and drinks with my theatre group followed by Shakespeare in the Park?"

He texted back immediately. "I love you in the park."

To which I replied. "I take it that is a yes?"

"Yes."

"Meet me at my hotel room after you get off work. I'm going to do laundry now."

"You don't need clothes. I prefer you naked."

"Ditto."

"Good, see you naked later." I laughed and felt my face heat as I turned my attention to Marco's inquisitive glare.

"Okay, Marco. We're in."

"Good. I can size him up," he said with narrowed, pale-green eyes.

"No interrogation! I expect you to be on your best behavior." I shook a finger in his direction.

His eyes opened wide and a naughty expression graced his face. "I don't think your park man would appreciate me showing off *my best behavior* to him."

I laughed then pulled a straight face. "I'm serious.

Behave!" Standing and thanking him for brunch, I kissed his cheek before we strolled out the door in opposite directions. Marco had a meeting and I had a bag full of laundry awaiting me.

Every day I walked home from Drake's home, dumped my dirty clothes on the floor, cleaned happily, aching body, worked on my highly anticipated project, headed to the theatre, and in between, had lunch with my man. When night time rolled around, I was back in the house and arms that belonged to Drake and the cycle played out. The result was a heap of clothes, and though he had insisted I use a service or do my laundry at his home, I didn't mind using the laundro-mat/coffee bar. It was a charming place to wash clothing. The couple who owned the place were delightful, offering to wash and fold laundry for patrons, but I enjoyed spending time in the place. Grabbing my soiled apparel off the closet floor, I shoved it into two pillow-cases then tossed my reader into my bag and headed out.

Walking in the front door, I loved the coffee smell paired with a clean, fresh laundry scent. The enchanting surroundings, mixed with the hum of soft music throughout the place contributed to the relaxing atmosphere and I looked forward to wash day. Some days I liked to sit on one of the black and white stripe leatherette upholstered sofas, in front of their turquoise tumbler washers and dryers with glass front, watching the clothes go round and round. Today, I chose to sit in a bistro-like section with a coffee and a book. However, I couldn't focus. I tried to read, but my mind wandered to Drake's words, "I love you in the park." He loved me? Or he loved me in the park? Mmmm... I loved him in the park too... No, that wasn't right... I just lusted after him. As my mind jumped between his words and Marco's, I must've looked like an idiot sitting with a big grin on my face. As soon as my clothes were clean and folded, I hurried back to my hotel. I texted Drake that I was ready for him. I couldn't wait to see him.

In the matter of thirty minutes time, I opened the hotel door sans clothing to *my* very handsome and excited man, who filled me with pleasure. I was perfectly content to skip the meet up and stay in bed for the rest of the night with his beautiful cock buried deep inside of me. Drake, on the other hand, was ready to go out and promptly tossed me over his shoulder then headed for the shower.

Dressed in a tank top and long skirt, minus panties as requested, we walked hand-in-hand to Finale Bakery and Desserterie at the Park Plaza. We were the last to arrive and it appeared the crew and a few cast members had already begun plying themselves with appetizers and bottles of wine. Marco had Kimee on his lap and she looked more than tipsy. I promptly introduced Drake to everyone before finding a seat. They were all cordial. By the time I got to Marco and his island tart, she was licking her lips, undressing Drake with her eyes right in front of me and then she opened her mouth. "You really know how to pick them. Damn! That new man of yours is fine! Thanks for leaving this one with blue balls for me to take care of the other night." She then twisted her fingers in Marco's hair and planted a big loud smack on his lips.

Drake turned and looked at me. I was still in shock and stared back at him until the bimbette opened her mouth again. "Oops, I guess he didn't know you were her boyfriend, Marco." We both turned our attention to her. Marco laughed, winking at me.

"Sofa was never my girlfriend, babe. Just a friend with benefits."

"Marco, I think you've had too much to drink." I tried to stay calm. I had never seen him act this way. Over the years we had both been around each other with dates and we acted like the normal friends I thought we were. Now, all I could do was stare at him in disbelief and wondered why he would say anything to a chick that was nothing more to him than a temporary toy.

"Hey, Sofa, don't be mad," he said, reaching his hand out to me.

Instantly, Drake calmly spoke up. "Don't fucking touch her."

Then as if Marco couldn't just shut up, he had to add fuel to the fire burning Drake's darkened, angry, lavender eyes to a shade I had yet to see. "Don't worry, dude, she hasn't been with me since you. Besides, she never gave a shit about me like…"

I had had enough. "Shut up, Marco… just shut up," I said and then grasped Drake's hand and pulled him away from the group. "Do you want to leave? I'm so sorry about this."

"You're fuck buddies with that guy?"

"We were, yes... over the years... from time to time."

"She said the other night. Was she telling the truth?"

"Yes, before you and I started anything, but after I had first seen you in the park. We were out having a drink and he came back to my room. We attempted, but I couldn't do it. Visions of you popped in my head and rather than use him, I made him stop. We have never been anything to each other... just a convenience."

"The room I just fucked you in?" Looking at me with dark and angry eyes, his tone was unfamiliar, one I had never heard before. When he said "fuck" on other occasions, it was sexy. But this was like fingernails, scraping a chalkboard. I grew ridged and nodded my head.

"You're checking out of that room tomorrow morning and you're bringing everything to my house."

"Drake..."

He cut me off. "Not another word about this." I stared at him, wondering what to say... wondering what was he thinking. He knew I wasn't a virgin. Yes, this was my fault. I could've told him about Marco, but Marco had never thrown me under the bus before so I never ever anticipated this happening. Drake hadn't spoken about past sex partners, why would I bring one up?

"Do you want to leave? We can leave right now.

Everyone would understand."

"No, I want to stay. Besides, your friend and his chick with the nice tits are leaving." I turned and saw them exiting the desserterie. I was saddened by the turn of events but relieved that there would be no more confrontations tonight with the remaining crowd. Walking back to the tables, I finished with introductions and we engaged in devouring some sinfully delicious desserts with champagne before we all made our way to The Commons to see the night's performance. By the time we entered the park area where the stage was set off of Tremont Street, there was a big crowd awaiting Shakespeare in the Park to commence. People were seated in low chair and others sat on the grass or on blankets; picnic baskets were all around. It made me think of our indoor picnics and that we should take ours outdoors, as well. I would have to plan something.

Situated off to the right side of the stage and too far away, as far as I was concerned, we watched the action begin. I loved Shakespeare. I had the best teacher in college who read the plays to the class and acted out scenes. He was far better than any cliff notes I ever read. This was my first time seeing Shakespeare performed outdoors, in a park, and it was the first time I had an orgasm while watching a play. Yes, sitting between Drake's massive legs, he causally slipped his strong hand down the front of my skirt. Luckily for me and the people around me, the performance was Richard III which included many dueling swords and lots of clanging to drown out the quiet whimpers that escaped my quivering lips.

We never made it to the end of the performance nor did make it completely out of the park before I was impaled by Drake's own magical sword. Part of me wanted to object as he pulled my skirt up and bent me over, but the other part of me was begging to be fucked. He was different than usual... rougher... he pulled my hair and thrust hard into me as his words between bites echoed in my ear.

"Say you're mine."

"I'm yours."

"I'm not a fuck buddy."

"No."

"No, what?"

"No, you're not a fuck buddy."

"Tell me again."

"You're not a fuck buddy."

"No the other part... you're mine."

"I'm yours... I'm yours... I'm yours," I panted wildly as his hand took command of my clit and he drove us both over the edge. I was his.

Chapter Seven

THE NEXT MORNING I was sore and wishing to stay in bed all day as he had proved to me over and over the night before that I was his. However, after claiming me one more time when he awoke, he hurried me to dress without a shower so we could leave. Grabbing a taxi back to my hotel. He was really making me check out. I thought for sure he wasn't serious but apparently, he was and with the stern look on his face—I didn't argue. Truth be told, I never stayed in my hotel room and I was perfectly happy to spend every waking moment in Drake's presence. I was addicted to him... I loved being with him.

"That's everything. Let's drop it back at the house and then you need to pack an overnight bag."

"Drake... I have to go into work tonight."

"Call in sick. We won't be back until Sunday night. I have business in Cape Cod and you are going with me. I'm not leaving you in the city alone."

Shit! Where did this possessiveness come from? Did he think I would fuck Marco if he was out of town? I stood with my mouth gaping open, watching as he gathered my things to give to the two bellhops. I had no desire to cause a scene so I remained calm and silent as we made our way downstairs. At the front desk, I checked out, paid my bill, thanked them for everything, and then gave one last wink to the concierge as we walked to a waiting taxi.

Sitting in the backseat, a lighter, happier, normal Drake reappeared. "Have you ever been to the Cape?" I shook my head and he continued. "You're going to love the Cape." Was he for real? He acted as if nothing had happened as he rambled about his plan to take me for a lobster lunch and show me one of his projects. I sat and listened and grew calmer by the minute; uncurling my nails that I had been imbedded into the palm of my hands. When we reached his townhouse, he and I brought my luggage upstairs.

Within an hour I had made arrangements, promised Lila a big bonus, packed an overnight bag, and seated myself into a Nara bronze Range Rover. Drake drove us out of the city. I'd seen on a map where Cape Cod was located and since we were leaving the city, along the water, I expected to see the Massachusetts coastline. I was shocked that our drive was nothing but greenery on either side of the highway. It looked like we were driving through a forest. I imagined this drive must be spectacular during the autumn. Something I would never see. Seeing signs for the Cape Cod turnoff I was excited to finally see the beach, but once again, no beach. The forest was gone and in its place was green countryside. Was there not a highway that ran along the coast? Giving up, I closed my eyes and slipped away to dreamland until I felt a pair of lips on mine, announcing we had arrived before capturing my mouth.

Opening my eyes first to gorgeous lavender ones, I then saw that we were parked in a dirt lot on a harbor. "Welcome to Hyannis, Sofie. Ready for some lunch?" That was when I realized we never had our customary Saturday morning breakfast with Sherry and that I was, in fact, quite hungry. I nodded. "Lobster?" Again, I nodded and received an amazing kiss before he got out and walked around to open my door. Slipping from the seat, Drake took my hand in his and walked me to the back deck of The Dockside restaurant. Seated under a navy blue umbrella on a bright sunny day, we watched ferries load and unload many passengers coming and going, to and from Nantucket and Martha's Vineyard. Drake ordered us two lobster plates and a bottle of white wine to sip while we enjoyed each other's company.

"What time is your appointment?"

"Not an exact time… this afternoon before the sun goes down."

"Is this a new architectural project?"

"Not exactly. I think you'll love it. As soon as we're done here, I'll show you one of my gems."

Leaving the harbor, we drove maybe a mile and a half down the highway, then turned down a private road to a gated area complete with a guard house. Waved through, we pulled into a gravel circular driveway, stopping in front of a two-story, shingled house in variegated shades of grey with white trim and big windows. Off to the side was a large, six-car garage with what appeared to be living-quarters above. The house looked old. He assured me it was not but it was made to look that way inside and out. From the outside, it was gorgeous. I couldn't wait to see the interior and fortunately, Drake didn't make me wait too long. Turning a key in the red-lacquered front door, we stepped over the threshold and were rewarded with an instant view of the Nantucket Sound through large, multi-paned, white wooden sliding doors.

"I love the view."

"Let me give you a tour of the house first, then we will go outside and enjoy the sun going down."

Pulling me up a wooden spindle staircase, Drake walked me from room to room. He showed me two master suites at opposite ends of the second floor, looking out to the water, and two guest rooms with ensuite bathrooms on the other side of the hallway. In the middle of all the rooms was a sitting area with a large flat screen TV complete with a remote control that closed off an enormous ocean view, bay window with black-out curtains for movie viewing. Making our way back downstairs, there was a state-of-the-art kitchen, a formal dining with a butler's pantry, housing the most gorgeous China dishes and crystal stemware; it looked vintage. Off of the dining room there was a formal living room we passed as we had entered the home. On the other side of the kitchen, there was a family room and a game room with access to the backyard through more multi-paned glass wooden sliding doors.

"The house is stunning. What amazes me is the mixture of ultra-modern furnishings and old world architecture; it blends perfectly. And the view... wow."

Opening one of the sliders, we walked out onto the stone-paved patio under a large white wood pergola that extended from one end of the house to the other. Two sitting areas with outdoor furniture flanked each end of the patio and in the middle was an outdoor dining area. Beyond the covering was a lush green, manicured lawn and in the middle, a rectangle in ground pool with a row of lounge chairs on one side, faced out to the Sound. Drake grasped my hand as we strolled to the edge of the property where a set of white wooden steps led down to a private sandy and rocky beach. We stood side by side, watching a ferry boat fade in the distance before walking back up to the house.

"Let's go in and see if we can find a nice bottle of wine." I saw a smile play on his face when I looked up into his dazzling lavender eyes.

"Wine? Your clients allow you to drink their wine?" He laughed, kissed my forehead, and guided me across the yard back into the kitchen. Cracking open a bottle of Pinot Noir from a glass front wine refrigerator, he poured two glasses and smirked the entire time. "You like being a naughty boy, don't you? Breaking the rules. Stealing wine." My words brought great laughter to my ears.

"I don't believe it is stealing when the house belongs to your father." He took a sip of wine, looking intently at me over the rim of the glass and I had to laugh.

"So... you built this for your father?"

"Yes."

"There was no appointment schedule for today, was there?"

I saw a boyish glimmer mixed with a bit of evil in those amethyst eyes. "No."

"You wanted to get me alone? Out of the city?"

He nodded, took sip from his wine glass, set it down on the granite surface, and prowled around the counter in my direction. I set down my wine and backed away from him. I could play his little game. I knew he liked public displays of affection so I continued out the open sliding door. I would give him what he craved. As he continued toward me, I stripped off the scarf I had weaved through the belt loops of my white, short shorts; a no-no item. When he was in reach, I grabbed his wrists, pulled them around him and tied them together tightly behind his back and watched a wicked smile spread from ear to ear. Stepping back, I removed each article of my clothing slowly and dropped them to the ground. There would be no discreet PDA today; we would be in full view.

Naked, I move in front of him; close enough to touch. "Not fair," he groaned, "I can't touch you." I just smiled, unbelted, unbuttoned, and unzipped his khaki shorts. I pulled them down his tanned, muscular legs.

Licking my lips, I grabbed a cushion off a nearby chair and fell to my knees. I was always so excited to take him in my mouth, to slide my lips, my tongue, and my teeth up and down his firm length, swirling and sucking his crown, taking him deep into my throat. God, his cock was glorious. So beautiful. The sounds that elicited from his lips drove me wild and made me sopping wet; I could feel it rolling down my thighs. His panting of my name encouraged me to suck even more vigorously as I cupped him with one hand and dug the fingernails of my other hand into his ass cheek, drawing him all the way in my mouth. I heard moans from both of us as he thrust forward and released. "Fuck... I'm one lucky bastard... your mouth is perfect... oh God, Sofie... you're the best."

Once he was properly licked clean, I picked up the cushion, stood up and backed to the nearest chair. Turning it around to face him, I returned the pillow to its original position and then I sat down on it and spread my legs out over the arms of the chair. I watched his tongue swipe over his eager mouth and I began to fondle my breasts. Kneading them with both of my hands, circling my rock hard nipples with my fingertips, I then tugged on my aching nipples as I stared at him and smiled. He smiled back with darkened eyes. I slid my hands down my torso, along the inside of my thighs, to my knees and then back up to settle them between my legs. I saw him swallow hard as I began to caress my slick lips. I was so wet, my fingers slid along perfectly, "Oooh, so good," I cried and threw my head back.

"Head up, Sofie. I want you looking at me. This is for me. No one else." Raising my head, focusing on his face, I brought one of my hands to my mouth and sucked my fingers, moaning. My naughty man was breathing heavily; I could see the rapid rise and fall of his chest. Time to throw him over the edge, see how much more he could take before he broke free and attacked me. Moving my hand back between my legs, I circled my hard nub then plunged two fingers into my pussy and began to fuck myself. I thought he would stop me, but no, he watched as I moaned his name. I had never been more turned on and it had never felt so good to fuck myself. If he asked me to stop now, I couldn't. Oh God, I had found a spot that I had never found before and suddenly, waves were rolling inside of my pussy. I could feel an amazing buildup and I moved faster, pushing harder into the yummy spot. Then it hit me full force and I screamed as a climax, like no other, ripped through my body. Liquid squirt out from between my legs. "Oh, Sofie... that was fucking amazing," I heard before I felt Drakes mouth engulf and lap my pussy. It was his turned to lick me clean. I enjoyed every swipe.

I don't know how I could still feel a wanting sensation after that but I did. And when Drake spoke, I knew we were on the same wonderful page. "Oh, Sofie... you're going to have to do that again for me... but right now, you have to untie me. As much as I liked watching that, I need to fuck you. I need to be buried in you." I smiled as he stood and turned around before doing as he asked.

I saw flames ignite in his lavender eyes as he swiftly pulled his shirt over his head. His body sent a shiver along my spine; it was truly a glorious sight. Quickly, he moved back to me, grasped my hair at the nape, tipped my head, and crushed his mouth on mine. Backing me until we were on the lawn, he turned me around to face the Sound and lowered me to the ground on all fours. We were on display; fully naked on the lawn. Anyone with a good pair of binoculars, on one of the various boats that cruised the shoreline to glimpse the homes of the rich and famous, could have a full show. The thought was somehow exciting. I moaned as he got behind me, spread my cheeks, and hammered me with his big, beautiful, erect appendage. He filled me up perfectly. God, he felt incredible inside of me. I couldn't get enough of him. I pushed back and as he drove forward. We moved into each other, screaming, panting, moaning out in the open; mating like animals, climaxing together. It was so powerful. Intense. I had to laugh when he howled his satisfaction, scooped me up, and jumped into the pool. That was one way to cool the moment.

While the sun went down, we swam, dunked each other, and made out in the pool like a couple of teenagers. It was so much and believe it or not, it was my first time skinny dippy with a man. Another first with the man I loved. I sighed, closed my eyes, and wished there would be many more firsts with him when the first star of the night twinkled in the sky. "Did you just make a wish, Sofie?"

"Yes… yes, I did." I turned to see him swim toward me and take me in his big, strong arms. My heart skipped a beat. Oh God, was I ever in trouble. He was my first love and soon he would be my first true heartbreak. How would I ever survive?

Chapter Eight

"GO OUT FOR ice cream or eat popcorn and watch movies naked?" Those were my two options once we christened the pool one last time. I'm sure anyone could guess my answer. Yes, we spent the night watching bits and pieces of two movies. If our lives depended on explaining the plots of either of the movies, we were surely doomed. Funny that we even attempted. At some point during the second film, Drake flipped off the TV and carried me to the master suite that belonged to him.

Awakened by a ray of sunshine and that lovely man spooning my backside, we climbed out of bed and leisurely made our way downstairs. Drake made us breakfast and then we got dressed; a bikini and a sarong for me and trunks for him for our day on the beach. Strolling down the shore, we looked at some of the distance houses and I received my architecture lesson of the morning. Back in front of the house, we built sandcastles. Wow! Could this hot man ever build with sand! When he was finally satisfied with his design, I took out my phone to snap a photo. I knew I would never be able to create something as beautiful and I never wanted to forget it. Just as I was focusing the camera, Drake took the phone from my hand and my simple picture became a selfie of us with our "Blaxton Castle," as he named it. Our first photo together.

Sandy and hot, we took a swim and enjoyed a siesta after an amazingly slow, loving fuck on a chaise lounge, poolside. I could've stayed in Cape Cod with Drake forever but reluctantly, we packed up and headed for Boston; stopping first for the best soft serve pistachio ice cream cone I'd ever had. I didn't even know soft serve came in any other flavor beside chocolate and vanilla. The place had a large selection of flavors and was packed with noisy, excited families, enjoying a sweet treat on a Sunday afternoon.

"I love seeing that," Drake said as he nudged me to look at little happy faces coated with ice cream.

"Me too. I love the laughter. It's Part of why I started going to the Frog Pond. Oops, looks like someone lost their ice cream," I said as a little boy stood—crying—looking down at a strawberry blob on the ground and an empty cake cone in his hand. Loved this place and the quick, friendly employee that presented the child with a new cone.

"That was close," Drake said laughing. Then without looking at me, his voice changed, a more serious tone replaced the silly banter. "Being an only child, I'd like to have a big family. What about you, Sofie?"

"I'd love to have two or three someday. No time now. I have a big project that I want very badly and a family doesn't fit in. The way my life is, a family may never fit my busy schedule." I answered so quickly. The words just kept coming and I noticed he became very quiet. A distance seemed to spread between us as we finished our ice cream . . . or maybe I was imagining it. I mean it's not like he was asking me to have his children. *His children.* Suddenly, I was sad; a lump formed in my throat and I had to look away as I felt tears fill my eyes. Someday he would be sitting here with his wife and children. I wished somehow it could be me. *Our* children... not just *his* children.

"Sofie... hey..." He bumped me with his elbow and I turned back to him. God, he was gorgeous. "You ready to go? Traffic will be horrible if we wait any longer." I nodded and grasped his outreached hand. I looked down at our connected hands as we walked to the car. I would miss that touch... that security... that bond. Only two more weeks. Four weeks had already passed so quickly, I silently prayed the next fourteen days would move at a snail's pace.

THE NEXT NIGHT, the theatre was dark so I decided to have dinner ready as Drake walked through the door. Very domestic. Ha! Not my usual modus operandi, but I wanted to do something special for him. I wanted this life with him. I wanted him. I wanted to be his. I was lost in our "forever" daydream when I was startled by *my*

handsome man, moving my hair aside and biting my neck. "Mmmm... you taste so good, Sofie. Whatever you are cooking, smells divine... I could get used to this." I moaned, thinking, *so could I*.

Shutting off the range burners, I turned into big, strong arms and he crushed his mouth to mine. I was ready to throw dinner out the window and let him take me right there on the counter... on the floor... wherever. Breaking the kiss, I turned my attention back to our meal as he stepped back, removed his tie, and rolled up his sleeves. I smiled to myself as his tanned skin became more visible, reminding me of our time in the sun on the Cape.

"I noticed the table was set in the dining room." All at once, my naughty thoughts fizzled and my back stiffened at his words. Had I overstepped my boundaries?

"I hope you don't mind. I used the China, crystal glasses, silverware... and linens I found in the glass cabinets."

"They are yours to use, Sofie. You are to use and do whatever you want in our home, darling. Everything is yours." He moved closer to me and kissed my cheek. "Let me help you."

I didn't know what to say so I just continued to move about plating our dinner. Since we arrived home yesterday, everything had changed to ours: our house, our bed, our kitchen. I had already been playing house with Drake for a few weeks but things seemed different between us with all of my things now installed in his townhouse. Before, my clothes and toiletries had remained in an overnight bag. Looking around for my things, Drake informed me that the right side of the walk-in closet was now mine. Stepping inside the magnificent space that could easily be featured in *Elle Decor Magazine*, I saw some of my garments hung up, while others had been put into drawers. My shoes sat proudly displayed on impressive racks. It looked so permanent and felt so right, but it was only temporary. I sighed, knowing it would be over before long.

"Sofie… Sofie… you alright?"

Nodding my head, I looked up into two dazzling, lavender gems and smiled. "Yes, I'm fine." I reached up and stroke his lightly stubbled face. "Let's eat. Help me get things to the table."

"Of course. It smells heavenly. I'm sure it's delicious." I thought he was positively delicious as he kissed my hand before he began to assist me.

Seated in upholstered grey tweed chairs at a large rectangular mahogany wood table under a rather modern dark, pewter grey and crystal chandelier, Drake opened wine after looking at the bottle. "Pinard Vineyard. Very nice. I've been meaning to try one of their boutique wines." Pouring a glass for each of us, he gave a little toast, thanked me for a delightful dinner, and told me about the wines of the Pinard Vineyard. He was ever so charming and informative. I could listen to him *forever*. There was that damn word again. I really needed to get it out of my head. Our time together was ticking away.

After a wonderful meal, we cleaned the dishes... actually, he cleaned everything while I served up dessert that we ate in the kitchen. "I have surprise for you." Putting his arm around my waist, he walked me out of the kitchen and upstairs. "Mmmm... I think I'm going to like this surprise."

As we bypassed the second floor, I was not certain what he had in mind. "Hmmm not where I was thinking," I sighed and Drake laughed as he guided me into his office/library. Immediately, I saw art supplies on the desk top. I moved forward to look more closely at the generous gifts he had purchased for me. Running my hand over a large leather portfolio sitting on the floor, next to the desk, I asked, "When did you get all of this?"

"Today at lunchtime. When I said I had a meeting. I hated lying to you but I wanted to surprise you... like you surprised me with dinner. I brought everything upstairs quietly when I saw you weren't in sight. I smelt the food and wanted to go to you immediately, but I forced myself up the stairs. By the way, I didn't like my lunch hour spent without you. Nothing beats you and your picnic basket in my office."

Grinning, I moved away from the desk. "I missed you today, too." Angling within his grasp, our clothes were quickly discarded and the office was properly christened.

OVER THE NEXT week, I took full advantage of the office every day. I had taken over his desk that had a fabulous feature; the top actually lifted at an angle and turned into a drafting table. What was once a neat space, was now covered with erasers, graphite, and colored pencils. Drawings were spread all over the room. I could see myself working in this space while kids played with toys on the floor before graduating to reading books. I thought about Drake visiting me; sharing a cup of coffee from the DeLonghi machine he installed in the library for me, and maybe a little playtime. What was wrong with me? I needed to get these thoughts out of my head. The theatre would be dark for good very soon. Then I had to go back to L.A. with my drawings in hopes of wowing my director friend and the producers. That needed to be my focus. I had worked too hard to give everything up now. I truly had no idea how Drake felt about me. I just knew he liked to be with me for the time being.

During the last running week of the production, Drake accompanied me to theatre. He took in the show a few nights from backstage and one night we sat amidst the fellow theatre patrons to watch the play. A couple nights we went out with some of the cast and crew after the night performances and Drake fit in perfectly. They loved that he schlepped us to some seedy, non-tourist bars. Even Marco warmed up to him, and apologized to both of us. He admitted he was jealous and had never seen me truly care for someone. All was good in my little world for the rest of the gig.

One of our last nights, sitting with the group at a high, long table in a dark bar, drinking and eating salty, fatty appetizers while some drunk people sang karaoke, I heard a very familiar voice shout out. "Blaxton? Is that you, man?"

"Hey, Dave!" Drake was off of his bar stool and embracing my director friend.

Slipping off my seat, I joined them. "David, what are you doing back in Boston?" Then I looked between the two of them. "Better question; how do you two know each other?"

"Drake worked on a couple of my student films. Then this dumbass decided he wanted play with building blocks instead of being a great actor."

They laughed, slapping each other on the back and began to reminisce, ribbing each about their old film school collaborations. I sat back and half listened in shock. Was it ever a small world! I came back into focus when I heard my name mentioned.

"Dave, how do you know Sofie? Please tell me you didn't date?"

"Oh, hell no, she wouldn't give me the time of day. She wanted nothing to do with what she calls *the boys club*. She set me straight right away and we became fast friends. She even introduced me to my wife. I guess I owe her." He laughed. "Hopefully, Sofie will be taking on my next big project... Hopefully she can handle working with me for a year. Did she pick your brain about architecture?"

"No," he said looking at me with a curious stare. I changed the subject with a casual comment and their conversation turned comical once again. We spent the rest of the night laughing.

THE NEXT DAY, the inquisition began after a mind-blowing morning in bed. Drake called in sick. We ended up closing the bar and stumbling into a taxi for home in the wee hours of the morning. We both needed some extra sleep and recuperation time. Curled up together, on the sofa with steaming hot cups of much needed coffee, we talked about the events of the night before.

"So architecture wasn't your first choice?"

"No. I fell into it. My father wanted me to go into the family biz. He owns an art auction house here in Boston. He suggested I major in art history and enrolled me in the UCLA program. I took classes about art, architecture, and sculpture. I was drawn to architecture after taking an Italian Renaissance class with an amazing professor. Then I had the opportunity to spend three months in Florence, Italy and when I came back, I announced my desire to change majors to architecture. The following school year, I transferred to another California school with a great architecture program."

"Interesting. I went to UCLA, too. Film school. That's where I met David. He was always trying to get me to do work in front of the camera. I had no desire. I liked setting the scene, the emotions... the overall feel. There are very few women in production design, but it's the job I really want. I know the competition is steep, but they are willing to look at my work... willing to consider me. I have to pitch against the Hollywood boys club. The project requires some architectural models. That is probably my biggest obstacle. That's why David asked if I had picked your brain."

"Perhaps you could use me. I love being used by you." There was that stunning grin.

"Ha!" I laughed. "I do love using you."

Then the expression on Drake's face shifted. "I'm serious. You really can ask me for help."

"You need to be a union man."

"Well... I actually did some acting while in college, remember? For Dave. It earned me a SAG card."

"You're still a member?"

"Yes, I keep up on my dues. I'm an academy member. I went from student films to paid union films. I had a couple bit parts. No leading roles."

"So you gave up acting to be an architect?"

"Yes, I did. It was fun. But like you, I like to design... to build... to see my vision come to life. No pressure, but if you want help, just say the word. I will be at your beck and call." I knew he was sincere and I told him I would keep his offer in mind, but really, I didn't want to talk about work; I wanted to enjoy every moment savoring each other.

Our time together was drawing to a close, limited to a few short days. I got up every morning with him; no more sleeping in. We drank coffee and then I would meet him every day for lunch with a picnic basket in hand. After work, we usually shopped for grocery items to cook or barbecue. Then for the rest of the night we remained wrapped around each other.

On our last night, we made our way to the North End for dinner. Neither of us was very hungry and decided to share a dish of linguini and clams along with a bottle of Chianti. Our evening was quiet and somewhat tense. There was so much I wanted to say, but I couldn't. Our brief relationship had been amazing and there was no reason to spoil it with tears and emotions. It was what it was—a summer fling. That was what it was, right? No, that was not true for me. It was my first time experiencing true love... first love... a love so special that I would cherish for the rest of my life. "You sure have a big smile on your beautiful face, Sofie. What are you think about?"

"I'm thinking about what a perfect evening this has been so far and how it would be really fabulous if we stopped off at Mike's for gelato, and pastry for the morning." He took my hand, kissed it and looked me straight in the eyes before pulling me out of the restaurant. "Whatever you want, Sofie... you can have whatever you want... just name it."

I wanted to scream, *"I want you! Only you! Every day. You!"* Instead, I laughed and let him treat me to yummy dessert. The next morning, I remained strong and said goodbye to him at the airport.

As the plane taxied down the runway, the tears sprang free and never stopped falling until we touched down in Los Angeles. I didn't mean for it to happen. I was always good at treating travel relationships casually. But never had I been so in tuned. So involved. So enthralled. So connected. So awakened. So in love. Yes... maybe I did love him. A pain in my chest had increased daily, knowing I was leaving soon. We were successful, career-oriented people, living opposite sides of the country. We could never last. Yet, I still questioned myself. Why did I let him in? I loved being with him. He was interesting. Smart. Funny. Oh... how I would miss everything about him...

His smell.

His touch.

His voice.

His taste.

His look... those lavender eyes.

Chapter Nine

D RAKE...
   She's gone. I let her go. The only woman I have ever loved. I let her go.

I drove her to the airport. It was surreal. I was functioning completely on autopilot. I hugged her. I kissed her goodbye. I wished her all the best. My last words were "let's keep in touch" and "text me when you get home." I treated her like a friend... a relative... a stranger... What the fuck was wrong with me? I should've told her I loved her... I should've told her we could make this work, but I couldn't. I just couldn't...

Returning home, walking through the front door, the emptiness struck me. The blow to my chest was swift, real, and oh so painful. I loved having her in my home... our home... our bed... I could no longer think of my townhouse as mine; it was ours. At least I wanted it to be ours. Her presence seemed to linger everywhere. I could see her in every room of this big, lonely miserable house. The house loved her in it. I loved her in it. I loved her. I loved her the moment I saw her at the Frog Pond. Why had I wasted so much time? I should've approached her or, at the very least, I should've moved her in the very next day after I carried her home in my arms from the park. The park that now taunted me.

Being without Sofie, I stopped walking through The Commons on my way home from work. My chest ached every time I strolled by the watering hole. I knew she wouldn't be there and I couldn't bear to see her usual bench empty. The first day I saw her had been a shitty day at the office. Things weren't moving smoothly on our Hong Kong project and I was trying to avoid a trip. I really needed to hear some laughter, so I made my way to the Frog Pond. Finding an empty bench, I took off my jacket and rolled up my sleeves and sat down to watch kids splashing and playing in the shallow water. The sights and sounds brought back wonderful memories of my youth. I was so happy I had stopped by and then I got more bad news; I was definitely going to have to fly out of the country. When I finally got off the phone, I didn't think even the pond could sooth me, but then my life changed forever. A vision of loveliness captured me; a honey-blonde haired woman with long, slender, tanned legs and a slim, curvy body. She was absolutely fucking breathtaking… gorgeous… and looking my way.

Now, I was sitting alone in my office that held scrumptious memories of our lunches together, looking at a photo of us. The one and only photo I had of my beautiful Sofie. I had two copies printed and framed. One sat in my office and the other one, next to our bed. Why didn't we snap more photos together? All I had was us in Cape Cod with our sandcastle. Thankfully, I had texted the photo, after I snapped it, to my phone or I wouldn't even have that.

Rubbing my thumb over Sofie's lovely face, there was a knock on my door and then my father appeared. "Damn! You look like shit!" were the first words that escaped his mouth.

"Thanks. Nice to see you, too." I replaced the photo on my desktop then turned my attention to my father as he pulled up a chair and sat. "What brings you here?"

"I was dropping off a catalog to a couple firms. Big auction coming up. Thought I'd pop in and see my only child. Haven't seen much of you lately. What the hell have you done to yourself? What's her name?"

There was no reason to deny or sugarcoat why I looked like I hadn't eaten… hadn't slept because I hadn't been able to do much of either. I also knew my father would drag it out of me, so I came clean and uttered the word that had contributed to the new look I was sporting, "Sofie."

"I see," said my father as he reached for the frame I had just placed on the corner of my desk. "She's quite beautiful." I sighed as he replaced the photo to its place. "Spill it." That is exactly what I did. I gave my father the PG-version of our brief, but intense and now painful, encounter. As always, my father had the solution. "Meet me Saturday morning at the diner and then you and I will do some rowing on the Charles. Clear your head. Get you thinking straight again, son." Then he stood, straightened his custom tailored suit jacket and tie before striding out of my office, leaving me with thoughts of the river and Fourth of July fireworks with *my* Sofie.

EQUIPPED WITH OUR picnic basket filled with fried chicken, homemade potato salad, and a variety of fruit Sofie had me cut up for Sangria and snacking, we made our way to my father's yacht club. There, he housed his 60-foot yacht and my Chris-Craft Corsair 36, a thirtieth birthday gift from my father. She was a beauty; a navy blue hull with a red stripe, cream deck from bow to stern with teakwood inlaid slants and a skylight on the forward deck that lit the galley and salon below. While my luxury, closed-deck cruiser was a beaut, she was no comparison to the woman in a leopard string bikini who sunned herself on the cream and tan upholstered seating.

Cruising along the Charles River all afternoon, watching her incredible body, had me hard as a rock. As soon as the sun went down, while we waited for the fireworks to start, I reached out and untied my beautiful package, watching scraps of material hit the deck. I continued my gaze as she grabbed a red, white, and blue decorative pillow, tossing it on the deck between my open thighs. I quickly discarded my shorts and that gorgeous woman, with just the right amount of teeth, tongue, and lips, sucked my cock. I gathered her sun-golden hair in my hand, pulled it to the side, and watched as two pale-green eyes glanced up at me. She was so fucking sexy with my erection slipping in and out of her lush mouth. It didn't take long for me to totally lose full control and explode. I loved how she drank it all in and licked any lingering drop. Fuck! She was so hot!

Sliding her to the floor of the deck we made out like teenagers on cushions until shooting flames lit the night sky. Sitting up, I pulled Sofie onto my lap and impaled her with my cock; I had never watched fireworks buried in such a glorious pussy that held me so perfectly. We never left the river that night. As soon as we docked, we christened the inside of the salon until the sun was starting to come up. I couldn't get enough of her. We couldn't get enough of each other; as soon as we would finish we were ready for another adventure. Exhausted, we finally fell asleep and never emerged from the cabin until late afternoon. The happy memories of that day made my chest burn and ache, knowing I would be tortured this weekend while rowing with my father on the same fucking river.

Not only would the memories kill me, but first, I was to get an earful from Sherry since my father insisted on breakfast to start fattening me up.

"Lavender Britches, eat up," she said as she sat a plate of eggs Benedict before me. I hadn't been into the diner since Sofie left. "What are you doing, dahling? Why are you torturing yourself? That girl loves you. Why don't you go after her?"

"I can't, Sherry. Not that simple. She has a dream. She deserves to be happy and fulfill her every desire." I hung my head and finished my breakfast. Walking out, Sherry gave me a big hug and kiss on the cheek, assuring me that she envisioned Sofie and I would get back together. She said we were destined for each other. I hoped, somehow, she was right and I hoped that rowing would somehow clear my head as my father said it would.

However, crewing with my father wasn't any easier. He couldn't leave well enough alone. He grilled me until I gave him the complete lowdown. How I took her to the Cape and moved her into the townhouse. I shocked my father.

"Wow. This is serious. I've never known you to let any woman into your personal space."

He was right. He had never known me to have a real relationship with a woman; even a short one, like with Sofie. Because before her, there had never been anyone I wanted permanently. I had never had a woman stay in my home nor ever taken one to the beach house. I had never spoken of a particular woman and of course never brought one to meet him… sadly, not even Sofie.

Oh my beautiful, beautiful Sofie. "I've never loved a woman before."

"Well, you may never find another one like her again. I know you're being noble but, son, there has to be a solution. I've never seen you look and act so down. Then again I've never seen you give up and not go after what you want. What can you do?"

"Nothing…"

"I don't know, Drake. I think the old saying always rings true..." I look intently at him as he paused. "If there's a will, there's a way." I hoped he was right. I needed to put my thinking cap on.

BACK AT WORK Monday morning, I was happy that I had projects to work on to fill the void in my daily life. I was also a little brighter after chatting with my father and being in touch with Sofie on Sunday afternoon via a few phone calls then a text this morning as I walked to work. It was not the kind of communication I longed for... I desired, but it was better than nothing. We made no promises... no plans but talked about maybes. Actually, lots of them: *Maybe I'll get a break and be able to see you. Maybe I can fly out. Maybe we can meet halfway.* Too many maybes.

I wanted her to be successful and, above all, happy. She was going to be in L.A. mainly, *getting all her ducks in a row* she said, laughing, and remarked how she missed the ducklings in the park. She was going to be working hard to secure the production designer position for David Maxsam's film. Her assistants were collecting resumes; she would be reviewing and gathering her team. I thought I heard a smile in her voice and though it was killing me, I was so proud of her for striving to capture her dream.

I told her that I was finishing a building in Boston. I

had a couple trips I needed to make to Hong Kong. We talked about dates that I could make a stopover so we could meet up: one, she would be off on a location scout with the director and cinematographer. The other time, she was going to be in New York for her friend's Broadway opening. She had hoped I could meet her in NYC or maybe she could pop up to Boston to see me. No, it didn't appear that things would work out for us and I would remain on the other side of the world longing to be between her legs. It appeared that our relationship would remain a hot summer encounter to remember—nothing more. Or was there a solution, as my father claimed? What could I do? It would have to be me. Could I sacrifice for her?

Yes... Yes, I could... I meant what I said, "I would do whatever she wanted..."

END OF AWAKENING TO YOU, PART 1

Awakening

to You...

in LA

Fifi Flowers

Champagne Girl Studio

Chapter One

SOFIE

WHEN BOXES, FILLED with my belongings, were delivered today from Boston, I felt the air suddenly whoosh from my body. My knees threatened to buckle; I was back to square one. Alone. Alone. Alone. I had heaven—I threw it away. The tears streamed from my eyes and all of the emotions that struck me when I landed at LAX came rushing back to the surface. I was back to my list of what wasn't said:

There was no "goodbye."

There was no "stay with me, Sofie."

There was no "come with me, Drake."

There was nothing… nothing…

We said nothing to each other; we kissed, we hugged, we waved.

"Text me when you arrive." The last words I recall from Drake's beautiful, full lips.

The plane ride was a blur. Landing was a blur. I had walked off the plane in an absolute fog, but at least I remembered to switch the airplane mode off of my phone. It instantly chimed. Of course, I had hoped it was

Drake. No. It was a text message from my ride… my ride that would not be. My sister Gracee informed me: "In San Fran, tied up in an amazing deal. Sorry not able to pick you up. Thought I would be home by now, but new client is proving to be a handful. Will explain when I have time. Sorry. Miss you. Love you, *SofaPillow*. Talk soon." Damn! I could've really used her advice… her ear… Non-commitment Gracee may not have the best answers, but at least I could've cried on her shoulder.

Gracee and I had always been close; born only twelve months apart. She was the *rhythm method baby*, and I was the *you can't get pregnant as long as you are breastfeeding baby*. "Ha!" was the answer to those two notions. My parents always called us their "lucky girls," despite their unlucky birth control methods, because after us, they were never able to conceive again. Being so close in age, along with the fact that our mother dressed us alike, people thought we were twins. We may have looked similar, but we were worlds apart. She was structured and business oriented. I was creative and undisciplined. After graduating from high school, she went straight into the real estate field. Working hard, she built her own empire by the time she was twenty-nine years old. I went off to college to find myself. I took my time trying different avenues in the art world until film school captured my attention. However different our make-ups were, we were forever gabbing whenever we got together; as often as possible. I hoped whatever was keeping her captive and away from me today, was something fabulous.

Shaking my head, I tucked my cellphone into the pocket of my maxi-skirt, squared my shoulders, and continued through the terminal. Traveling with only a carry-on bag, I made a beeline through baggage claim, searching for a taxi queue. I knew it could be a small fortune but I was definitely in no shape to share a shuttle van with strangers. Also, I had not made a limousine reservation. To my surprise, a tall, muscular, uniformed man, standing in front of the exit, held up a sign with the words "Sofie James" scrawled across it. Gracee to the rescue. Thank goodness. I couldn't be too mad at her for her last minute notice.

Introducing myself to the driver, he promptly grabbed my black leather, satchel-style, overnight bag. I followed the man, sporting a chauffeur's cap, to a waiting, black town-car. Seated in the backseat, I gave him my address, and we in engaged in small talk. The chit-chat was comforting as I wasn't ready to text Drake yet. The driver told me about the mild summer weather that they had been having in Los Angeles. He said the weather channel anticipated that it would probably heat up with the beginning of fall. "Ha!" I thought. Typical California weather. I remembered, as a kid, that the first few weeks of school were always unbearably hot; many of the classrooms lacked air conditioning. Feeling a bump in the road, I realized I had either stopped listening or he had stopped chatting. I'm not sure which happened first, but my thoughts ran to our lack of true seasons, and the variety that were experienced in Boston. Seasons. I wanted seasons... I wanted Drake in the fall, winter, spring, and summer.

Daydreams of changing leaves, snow, and new blossoms accompanied me on the long traffic-filled ride. Before I knew it, the front garden of my California bungalow was in view. A quaint 1920s heather grey, stucco cottage with stark white trim and natural stone façade. My two bedroom, two bath house was located in Toluca Lake, close to theatres and film lots; a perfect location for me. Or at least . . . it once was.

Parked, the chauffeur opened my door, extended his hand to help me out of the car, then walked me and my bag to the door. Unlocking my black lacquer, glass-paneled front door, I set my bag down inside on the dark chocolate colored, wood-planked floor. I pulled out my wallet to tip the driver. "Oh no, Miss James. Mr. Blaxton took care of everything." Those few words hit me like a Mac truck, causing me to stumble on my feet. Squeaking out a "thank you," he tipped his hat, then strode back to his shiny black car at the curb. Turning around, I stepped over the threshold, shut the door, walked straight to my bedroom, undressed, dropped my clothes, and entered an empty shower stall. As much as I wished to keep Drake's scent on my body, I needed to relieve the tension that had me on edge with the help of strong, pulsating jets of water. Refreshed, I slipped on yoga pants, a t-shirt, secured my hair in a ponytail, grabbed a bottle of red wine, a glass, and deposited myself on a comfy, rattan, sectional sofa to unwind... to cry.

That was two weeks and a few, nonchalant, phone conversations with Drake ago. Time hadn't healed my wounds—I was still feeling the same ache in my chest. Turning on some sappy loves songs, sorting through these packages, it made me think about the *complete package* I left behind. For two glorious months, I had greatly enjoyed being wrapped in the strong arms of an extremely kind… incredibly handsome man. Every moment with him had been wonderful… magical. I had no complaints. He never gave me a reason to… No, I couldn't recall a single imperfection. What were his downfalls? I was sure he had some. Perhaps if our relationship was a permanent situation, I would find some. No one was perfect, but he was damn close.

When I finally got to unpacking the last box, my heart nearly stopped beating. Right before my eyes, neatly folded, was Drake's silk robe. His musky, sensuous, manly scent wafted up, hitting me full force. I breathed *him* in deeply. Reaching down, I ran my fingers gently over the charcoal-grey fabric. My thoughts ran to the first time I saw him wearing it. It was a Sunday morning. I stretched, yawned, and rolled over to see *my sexy man,* wearing the pinstriped robe while reclined against a stack of pillows, reading *The Beacon Hill Times*. With one leg up, the silky fabric fell open, making me privy to a wonderfully muscular calf and thigh. Casting my gaze farther up his hard body, a gap showed off a strong chest. Yum! I smiled, licking my lips.

"Do you like what you see, Sofie?" I was caught

lusting.

Naked, I crawled out from beneath the light, summer coverlet, reached under the silky robe and firmly stroked his visible hardness, I asked, "Reading something exciting?" Smiling, I bit my bottom lip then replaced my hand with my mouth.

Tossing the paper on the floor, Drake placed his hands behind his head as he watched my lips slip over the crown of his cock. "Looking at something exciting." He winked at me as I happily continued to pleasure him, licking his pre-cum with a swirling motion. Then running my tongue along his shaft, I grazed my teeth down his full length, taking him into the back of my throat. "Oh… so good, Sofie, but I need to feel you pulsing around me while I'm buried deep within you." Two strong arms, reached down and pulled me up, causing me to straddle his body. I greedily accept him.

God, how I missed him. I moaned, thinking about how good he felt snuggly cradled inside of me. Stripping off all of my clothes, I needed to feel a part of him… to have his scent around me. Pulling the silky robe from the box, I slipped my arms into the sleeves, wrapped it around me, and tied the sash in a bow. Crossing my arms over my chest and rubbing them, I closed my eyes, hugging and sighing to myself as I imagined that it was Drake holding me. Would I ever feel him again or was this a parting gift? A memento of what was? Or was it a hint of what could be?

Maybe I was reading too much into it, I thought, as I

turned back to the last box. Then it hit me. No. I was right. There was definitely more to just a box of my things. These were not my things. There was an antique leather bound, empty sketch book, ready to be filled. A box of French, graphite drawing pencils with varying lead weights and thickness. A quill pen and some India ink pots. They were all charming art supplies, perfect for displaying on a shelf in my studio space behind my house. Gifts… he sent me gifts to be treasured. Would he ever see them, I wondered, as I put the items back in the box to take out to my studio in the morning. Then I noticed a large envelope, resting along the side.

Pulling the manila envelope out of the box, I folded back the flap and grasped a thick piece of parchment. Slipping it from the envelope, I flipped it over to see a drawing of me in Drake's bed. I was wearing the robe that now held me tightly. "Oh my God," I said as I realized the only time I had worn his robe. It was the day he carried me home from the Frog Pond, undressed me, and wrapped me in his grey robe. The thought of his beautiful, lavender eyes, watching me while I slept, stirred something deep in my core. The sketch was beautifully drawn; very detailed. It made my heart sing and ache, all at once.

Taking the drawing with me to my lonely bedroom, I curled up in my big, empty bed with the scent of Drake encompassing me. Tears streamed down my face. I told myself "this was it." I would allow one last night of waterworks… one last night to mourn the loss, and then

I needed to regroup… to focus. I had a career. A lifelong dream. It was so close this time. The brass ring was within my reach. It was my turn to shine… to conquer.

Chapter Two

DRAKE

WAKING UP THIS morning, I was disoriented; one too many crystal tumblers, filled with whiskey. Lying about in my bed, the scent of Sofie had my heart racing. Since she left, I'd allowed my sheets to be changed but not her pillowcase. Eventually, I would need to give in, but not yet. Scrubbing my hand over a beard I had grown since her departure, I thought of a naked Sofie, still asleep, in her own bed, on the other side of the country. The things I wished I was doing to her flooded my head. Overwhelmed by lustful thoughts, I decided to get out of bed. Padding across the room to the closet, now devoid of Sofie's summer dresses… her lingerie… her shoes… her presence, I grabbed for my robe. It was time to get back to my usual routine. And then it hit me—my robe was gone. I had overnighted it in a box filled with antique art items that I had purchased, for *Sofie's library*. Only, it wasn't her space anymore. But I saw her there every time I entered the empty room. I had hoped that, since she wouldn't be using them here, that she could enjoy them in her home. Looking at my robe tied around my waist, I unknotted it, and added it to the box. I wanted it to hug her… to hold her… to make her think of me… to long for me… To be honest, it was a constant, painful reminder of the first time I undressed her, cloaking her in my robe.

The memory of that day was vivid, imprinted on my brain like it was just yesterday. I was so scared as I scooped Sofie up in my arms after she struck her head on the park tree. First, I wondered if I should take her to the hospital, but then decided to take her to my home, across the street. I was happy that she was mumbling, occasionally blinking her eyes open and closed. Reaching my house, I unlocked the door and carried her straight up to my bedroom. Settling her on my bed, I called Rich, my doctor friend. Luckily, he answered, informing me that he was only two blocks away. He told me to watch her closely. That is was important to keep her warm. I noticed her soaking wet clothing. Feeling I had no choice, I decided to remove the completely drenched garments stuck to her shapely body. Pulling her up to a sitting position, I asked her if she could raise her arms, to my surprise she did. I gently tugged her top up and off of her, careful to not hurt the bump I felt on the back of her head. Then I unhooked her bra, as I silently whispered "God help me," as two of the most perfect breast greeted my eyes. I groaned, thinking about licking and biting her pert nipples. Shaking my head, I focused on slipping her arms into my robe, then removed her sandals. Reluctantly, I moved on, sliding her fitted skirt and panties down her slender, yet, curvy hips. "Oh, her body was amazing," I thought as I tossed the wet clothes to the floor, wrapped the robe around her, and tucked her inside of my bedcovers.

I wanted her so badly that day. I wanted her so badly every day. I wanted her to feel me around her. Images of her naked body stiffened my cock, painfully, once again as I headed for my walk-in shower stall. Washed, I toweled off and dressed, instead of reading the paper in my robe. Locking my front door, I grabbed the newspaper tucked in the door pull and walked to breakfast. No, not the usual place. I hated to do it, but I avoided Sherry, as well as Newbury Street. Not that other streets were easier to venture down, but I did my best to find places I didn't frequent with Sofie. I just couldn't bear them without her. I truly needed to get over these feelings or I was going to have to move to a new city. However, that was not an option.

AFTER OUR DAY crewing on the Charles River, my father had made a point to keep in daily contact with me. He insisted we meet for lunch as often as possible. Yes, my weight was going back up, thanks to his intervention. He asked my advice on several architectural pieces he was thinking about purchasing for his auction house. He even brought blueprints for a possible building project. It reminded me of when we lost my mother. He wanted to spend every moment he could with me. He called me daily on the phone. He was heartbroken, said it was his fault, that he was being punished. He thought it was unfair, she was younger; he should've gone first. He assured me over and over that he truly loved her. He confessed that he should've shown her more often. He regretted how he had hurt her. He never hold me how he hurt her, but I suspected it had something to do with another woman.

My parents met when my father gave a talk at my mother's college two months before she was to graduate. I was told, by my mother, that she was smitten while sitting in the front row, before the lecturer; a very handsome, suited man with lavender eyes. She said all of the girls were hanging on his every word. My father said he never noticed. He was immediately drawn to the pretty brunette who took her time gathering up her belongings; my mother. He asked her out for a drink and offered her a position in his auction house. She declined both. Three years later they ran into each other at an art event, this time she accepted a date, declined another job offer, but accepted a marriage proposal four months later. Their first years together were rocky. They fought over her working in a competitor's auction house, the fact that they were both traveling often, and never together. Finally, he gave her an ultimatum. She, in turn, gave him baby news.

My father never wanted children, especially not at his age; he didn't want to be an old dad. My mother told him, "then don't be." She went on to assure him that I was his chance to relive his childhood. That was exactly what he did. He was very attentive. Extremely active in all of my extracurricular activities. He got me into crewing, took me fishing, sailing, and taught me about the many ins-and-outs of running an art auction house. I agreed to join the family business and went out West for college to study Art History, before switching my major. While I was in my last year of architecture school, tragedy struck; my mother was fatally injured in a car accident and passed away. I came home, briefly, for the services. After a week, I then returned to finish up my senior year. After graduation, I went home to be with my father permanently, taking a position with a firm in Boston to be nearby. We have remained very close despite our forty-five-year age difference. He has acted more like a brother than a father at times, and even asked me to be his best man when he remarried a few years ago.

I was happy to hear from my father earlier in the day. Nothing seemed to be going right. I had tried to put my plans in motion that would allow me time to see Sofie, but my connection was off-the-grid, traveling to parts unknown. I received an invitation for steaks, wine, and cigars; a good diversion. My father's wife, Vivian, was out of town for the weekend so a little male-bonding was in order, according to my father. Dressed in casual attire, I slipped into a pair of tan leather loafers. I left my house, walked down Beacon Street, then turned up Walnut Street, heading toward my father's townhouse. Memories of *my* beautiful Sofie flooded my head. Even more so when I opened the gate to my father's secret garden, where I took great pleasures in her exquisite body.

I loved public sex with her, but I never wanted anyone to see us. When I took Sofie to the secret garden, twice, I knew my father and Vivian were gone on vacation. The house on the Cape was so secluded, it was rare to see a neighbor. But the excitement of being caught was there. The park, however, was risky... not smart, but that night I had to claim her... to mark her. Yes, we were lucky then, and on another evening at the local cinema. The night before, I had tried to talk her into letting me take her at *her* theatre but she wouldn't give in. However, the movie theatre was a very different story altogether.

Grabbing a couple bottles of water, a small bucket of buttered popcorn, and napkins from the concession stand, we found seats in the very back row of the darkened, empty theatre. Pushing up the armrest between our two seats, we snuggled up with my arm around her shoulder like a horny teenager about to make *the move*. We both laughed as I groped her breast slyly, forgetting all about the movie projected on the silver screen. Sofie was such a naughty girl leaning over the chair in front of me, exposing her bare bottom. I loved that she rarely wore panties. I moaned as I stroked between her legs. God, she was so wet! Slipping two fingers inside of her, I slid my moistened fingers from her clit to her rosette, to my surprise she backed into my fingers. Coating my fingers again from her wetness, I circled her opening, biting her backside before whispering, "Do you like this, Sofie?" She nodded, backing into my hand again. That was all the invitation I needed from *my sexy girl*. Unzipping my pants, I pulled her up, held her firmly around the waist, entering her with my cock and then my finger. Fucking her two openings, our movements grew frantic. We panted like two wild animals. Thankfully, the movie was action packed; loud enough to drown out our moans of ecstasy as we climaxed together. Shaking my head, I laughed, thinking that it was truly a miracle we didn't get caught.

"Hey... earth to Drake. Are you going to stand out there, admiring my garden or are you going to come inside?" My father asked, leaving the front door open as he briskly turned around, disappearing down a hallway. I laughed harder. If he only knew what had me staring... what I had done to Sofie in *his* secret garden. Walking in, I heard the martini shaker rattle. Following the sound, I saw clear liquid poured into two frosty glasses where skewered olives waited to be bathed. "Cheers," my father said, lifting his glass. I raised mine as well, clinking it to his. Nodding my head, I took a sip before my father instructed me to follow him.

Up a couple flights of stairs, we walked out onto my father's deck, off of a small kitchenette that was part of his family room. Opening the lid of a large stainless steel barbecue, I watched as he grilled two nicely marbled, rib-eye steaks. To my surprise, he reached down on the side of the barbecue grill and grabbed a handful of pastel Jordan almonds. I asked him what was up with those, I had seen them in his kitchen, on his bar downstairs, and in his work office the other day. Apparently, he had gone to a wedding where they were sitting on the table wrapped in tiny bags and he became addicted to them. He went out the very next day to buy several bags. Instantly, my thoughts ran to Sofie; she loved them, too. She bought a bag of them, weekly. She had told me they were considered a lucky gift to wedding guests as they symbolized: health, wealth, happiness, fertility, and longevity. I smiled to myself as I popped one of the almonds into my mouth.

"Where is your head tonight, my boy? Still with that girl... woman?"

"Yes. I can't seem to get her off of my mind... To be honest, I really don't want to."

"Well then, why don't you pop down to the cellar... get us a bottle of red wine. I just got a case of Pinard Bordeaux. Then meet me in the dining room and tell me what the hell you plan to do to get this woman back. Enough moping about—get off your fucking ass and make it happen."

I laughed, shook my head, and made my way down to the cellar. It was rare to hear my father use the "f" word. It usually meant he was fed up, upset, or deadly serious. I knew he was right; it was time to put my plan into action. I would get Sofie back... or die trying.

Chapter Three

SOFIE

B ACK TO MY routine, I began to pull all of my storyboards together. And with the help of Lila, I compiled possible crew members. I dragged my body out of bed to do yoga three days a week, plus walked my treadmill daily. I would've gladly thrown both of those forms of exercise out in lieu of contorting my body with Drake's. Also, for our walks along the streets of Boston. Oh, how I longed for moments with him; each morning I stretched out in my bed… every night I crawled into bed… anytime I was in my bed. Yet, time apart was clearing my brain, allowing me to focus… to daydream a little less. I had incredible memories, but reality had set in; my professional dream was getting closer every day. Production design was my destiny.

Though I hadn't made my decision to enter the film industry until a couple years into college, I had been surrounded by the industry. My parents had been involved in the movie business since I entered my teen years. My father's family had owned an automotive scrap and salvage yard since he was a little boy. He and his two brothers took over the business when their father died at a young age. The brothers loved old cars and began collecting them through the years. Broken down ones were their favorites because they could restore them. In doing so, their business expanded to car restoration. Many vintage cars remained in their collections but far more were sold. The silver screen connection happened when one of their roadster sports cars was sold to a well-known movie director producer. When the man came to the automotive junkyard to pick up the car, he was overwhelmed by the brothers' collection. He asked if they would consider loaning cars to be used in films. They loved the idea, the challenge. This new business expansion called for the brothers to purchase more surrounding land to build hangars that housed cars, auto body equipment, and tow trucks for transporting cars to sets. My father was the brother to oversee this new endeavor. I often tagged along.

I loved to visit the sets. The magic of creating the illusion fascinated me. Even the cars my father provided. To convey a certain mood, my father was often asked to paint some of the cars obscure colors. For example, he worked on a silly romance movie, featuring a very girlee character, where they requested a bubble gum pink MG sport-cars. That is exactly what they got. But if you ever looked carefully; the door jambs were often a different color. There were many things movie goers never knew; many cars didn't run... didn't have engines... didn't have window-shields or even windows, but they could sit and look the part. Long enough to give the film the look the director envisioned and the production designer helped bring to life.

Now was my time to contribute to a feature film. I was beyond ready. Everything had come together. It all felt right. I knew it was mine. I just had to sell myself to the producers. It was a miracle my nerves weren't on edge. That was thanks to being in contact with my director friend, David, almost daily since I had gotten back to LA. He liked what I had come up with but ultimately it wasn't completely his decision. He needed the producers to fund his project. I needed to convince them I was the best person for the position.

The day of my big meeting, I got up early to give myself time to focus on positive energy. As luck would have it, it was a nice, warm, sunny morning. Perfect weather for a little yoga stretch and mediation out on my teak deck which spans the whole length of my house. Pulling on a pair of black yoga pants along with a grey, black and white striped tank with hot pink crisscross straps, I opened two wood, sliding-glass doors off my master-suite and stepped outside. Upon hearing the waterfall that flowed into a koi pond, a lovely, calming vibe fell over me. I truly adored my overgrown, yet groomed back garden with vines, bamboo, and a variety of flora that provided a sweet smell in the air.

Turning on some relaxing music, I rolled out my lime-green mat. Moving through my favorite poses, I felt remarkable. I focused my mediation on attaining positive energy. Something I would need. *Today, things would be in my favor*, I silently chanted until I felt tension leave my body. Finished with my yoga techniques, I rolled up my mat to go prepare for my big day. I felt ready as I stepped into my natural-stone shower. I could only think of one other thing that could've made my morning better as I stood naked under the gentle rain of water.

Dressed in black slacks with a black and white striped Georgette blouse, I went out to my studio to grab my leather portfolio, courtesy of one absolutely gorgeous Bostonian man. As I was zipping it closed, memories, from the night that Drake had brought art supplies home and onward, flooded my brain. How many times had I look out to our frog pond with him inside of me? Over the desk? Against the window? Straddling him, seated in his leather office chair? Moaning softly, I closed my eyes. I could see his lavender eyes. I could almost feel his full lips on mine. My insides warmed, my juices flowed, my nipples tingled. I was just about to unzip my pants for some relief when my phone buzzed, reminding me I had somewhere to be. Grabbing the case, I started to exit my studio.

Looking at the screen, I saw that it was a text from David, and suddenly my day seemed to be on rocky ground. "Leave artwork at home. Not necessary. Come alone." *What the fuck did that mean?* I wondered, dropping the portfolio next to the door. Walking down the granite pathway, I went inside, gathered my handbag, keys, and headed for my prized convertible, Karman

Ghia, in the garage. Putting down the top, I pulled my hair into a ponytail, slipped behind the wheel, and maneuvered through the traffic.

"Shit! Shit! Shit!" I said, hitting the steering wheel, waiting for a red light. The closer I got, the more scenarios played out in my head from bad to worst.

What was about to happen?

Why was I still joining them if they didn't want me?

Why not cancel our meeting?

Were they going to offer me a lesser role?

Would I... Could I accept it?

By the time I arrived, I had myself so worked up. I was certain my dreams were doomed. What was wrong with me? I needed to get a grip. I needed to think positive. I could've been all wrong. Rolling up to the valet, I looked in the rearview mirror briefly to check my appearance, then exited the vehicle. Grabbing the ticket extended to me, I strolled in like I owned the fucking place. Walking into the dining room entrance, the hostess led me to a table occupied by four men, one of which was my good friend, David. I was relieved when he saw me, smiled, and introduced me as his production designer. I was in shock. I was thrilled. I beamed as he explained.

"Sofie, I told these gentlemen that I was extremely happy with your storyboards and the team you've assembled so far. They trusted my judgment, agreeing to take me at my word. Hence; the text, telling you to forget your portfolio. However..." He paused, rubbed his chin, and then continued. "We decided to bring in an expert for the construction part. Your structural ideas are great, but this film involves multiple model builds with special effects…"

"I could get someone." I offered not wanting to look like I couldn't find people to handle this project.

"Sof, we've already brought someone on board." I looked at him intently. "He's been working on the project for a few weeks. We were impressed after seeing his renderings and computer capabilities. The samples he sent us were amazing." I tried not to grimace, but I'm pretty sure confusion was written all over my face. He could've warned me, I thought, as he finished explaining. "It's a firm decision. Backers want him. I don't have to tell you we need the financial support."

"Yes," I said, shaking my head in disbelief as I gazed around the table of wealthy men. Then turning toward a seemingly nervous director who was looking at me wide-eyed, and biting his lower lip, I commented, "David, I understand perfectly." I hoped my voice was as monotone as I was attempting.

Relief immediately slid over his face, causing a glimmer of light to dance in his amber eyes. "Great. It will work… It will all come together, Sof."

I patted his hand, rewarding him with a smile I hoped looked sincere while thinking, "Damn! *Boys-club* struck again!" It will never change. Since film school, this is what I always had to deal with. I was told, "Be an actress… sew costumes… forget about production design." At least, I had finally gotten the position. Now, I had to be sure that I showed my crew—including the one undesirable—I was the one in charge.

Arriving home, after choking down, what turned out to be, a delicious lunch and productive, yet infuriating meeting, my phone began to ring. God, how I loved that ringtone. *Boston* by Augustana. Yes, it belonged to *my* Drake. Unfortunately, I was not in the mood. Declining his call, I texted him instead.

"Not good company tonight. Rant City. You don't want to hear it."

"What happened?"

"The fuckers went over my head. Behind my back. And hired a model expert. My concepts were good, but they wanted more details."

"Maybe it will work out better than you think."

"Just the *boys-club* bullshit continues. They could've let me interview candidates." Stomping into my bedroom, I kicked off my shoes, slipped out of my clothes, wrapped myself in Drake's silk robe, then flopped on the bed. "Sorry, how was your day? Better than mine, I hope."

"Actually, I'm pretty excited. New project. New challenge for me. Travel."

"That's wonderful Drake. I'm happy for you." I was happy for him... and then not. I wanted him to tell me he was miserable. I wanted to hear he needed me... longed for me.

"Sofie, I can tell you're down but I have a feeling it

will all work out. You got the job of your dreams. Don't let one little thing get to you."

Good that we were only texting and he couldn't hear that I yelled, "One little thing?! Ugh!" He didn't get it. He was a man. He had no idea how it was to work as a woman in a male-dominant industry. But there was no need to fight with him. He wasn't the enemy. "You're right. Besides, I will be the fucker's... the asshole's boss... Ha!"

"Do you know he's an asshole?"

"No." I texted with a sigh. I needed to change my attitude. "He could be a great guy, for all I know. I'm just mad."

"I know a good way to calm you down." I imagined a smirk on his handsome face. "Boston... no one..." started playing. I answered.

"What are you wearing, Sofie?"

I smiled, looking at the silk fabric that hugged my naked, pulsating body. "Your robe."

"Mmmm... what else?"

"Nothing."

I heard him groan, "Open the robe..."

I laughed while untying the sash. "What are you wearing?" I imagined his body sprawled out on *our* bed. I loved his hard body.

"...are you still there?" I missed his answer. I had tuned him out as I slipped my hand over my breasts, pinching my nipple, dragging my nails. I needed his teeth. I moaned. "I hear your whimpers, Sofie. God, I wish I was there, running my tongue down your skin. I bet you're so wet…" I could hear him breathing hard. I needed more.

Reaching next to my bed, I opened a drawer and pulled out the next best thing to his yummy, hard package. Then I asked, "Are you thinking about burying yourself in my wetness… stroking your beautiful cock?" I panted Drake's name as I slipped my favorite vibrating companion inside of me.

"Come for me, Sofie… oh… God… so close… You feel so good… FUCK… you're so fucking hot." As he commanded, I climaxed with him. He was right. I needed it. It did calm me… But, it made me feel empty… lonely… longing for the real thing. I wanted it; the real thing.

Chapter Four

DRAKE

M Y NEW PROJECT had me working my ass off. I was totally out of my realm with this job. It was a challenge unlike anything I had ever attempted. It had me shaking my head on several issues. Why had I decided to take on such a big adventure? I wasn't sure. Actually, that wasn't true. I knew why I did it. It was because of Sofie. If truth be told, I had to admit, the distraction was good for me. The days passed by more swiftly, but the nights were a killer as I inhabited *our* empty bed.

Occasional phone sex with Sofie didn't help. No, it made it worse. It was making me crazy. Yes, I could've jumped in, dated another woman. We had no agreement. No commitment. For all I knew, she was in someone else's bed. No, I didn't believe that, but I needed the real thing. Oh, how I wanted to feel her velvety walls pull me… hug me as I slid in and out of her warm pussy.

One Friday night, after work, I headed out with a few buddies to an old hangout of mine. While sitting at the bar, tossing back one beer after another, in sashayed a voluptuous female friend with long brown hair. "Hi, Drake… have you missed me?" Before I could respond two arms flew around my neck, glossed lips were planted on mine, and I felt a tongue flick over my bottom lip before she pulled away laughing. "Buy me a drink, sweetheart." Winking, she shooed my friend off of his stool then climbed up next to me. Prior to Sofie's arrival in Boston, Laney had been a convenient fuck—nothing more. I could call her up and pop round to her place for a little *relief.*

By the end the night, I had drank more than my body weight in alcohol. I knew it was time to leave. I was definitely going to feel like shit the next day. Half walking, half stumbling out of the bar, Laney was right alongside of me. There was no doubt about it, she was persistent. No harm sharing a taxi. I invited her in, and gave the driver her address. Stopping in front of her building, she reached over to place a kiss on my cheek. "Come up for a night cap," rolled off her lips as she cupped my pants where my boys sat. My body exited the vehicle, moving up familiar stairs with my cock dictating my every move. Settled on her sofa, I kicked off my shoes, leaned my head back, closed my eyes and it hit me that I really had had way too much to drink. I needed to get the hell out of there. My mind needed to get back in the game. "Gotta go," I said immediately as I heard her heels getting closer.

"Don't be silly," she whispered bringing a hand

across my chest, causing me to open my heavy lids. There she was, completely naked with her extremely large breasts and soft curvy body. Instantly, I thought of Sofie's fit, slender, toned body which caused me to moan and encouraged Laney to straddle me. My cock begged me to let *him* have her as she rotated her hips. Yes, *he* was betraying me; straining to meet her movement. She purred, "Someone is ready to play." Oh God, she was so right. I really fucking needed this. I needed the real thing. I closed my eyes again, feeling her push her tits into my chest. Rubbing them on me, she kissed my neck softly. Not animalistic. There was no biting like Sofie. She felt so wrong, but the sensations relayed to my lower brain were so right.

Climbing off me, she undid my pants. I lifted my ass for her. "No, no," my mind said silently, but my cock roared, "Hell, yeah!" Straddling me once again, sliding her wet cunt up and down my stiff shaft, I groaned out of ecstasy. Then regret hit me, realizing I let things go too far as I heard the rip of a foil package and felt the rolling of latex over my cock. Oh God, it was getting so real... too real... stroking followed by more sliding over my erection with her slick folds. Breathless words were slipping from her lips in a panting fashion. Her entrance was right there. I was ready to give in when she screamed, "Oh God," coming all over my wrapped cock. "FUCK!" I screamed inwardly. That was so wrong... so wrong. I was suddenly fully alert. My eyes flew open. I found my voice, "I can't. I can't."

"What do you mean *you can't*?" Laney pulled back, watching me run my fingers wildly through my hair.

I covered my face. I was ashamed of myself. I loved Sofie. How could I do this to her? "Sorry, Laney, I can't do this to Sofie." I tried to move her, but she gripped me tightly with her lush thighs. I could see by the redness and the scowl on her face that she was pissed.

"Who is Sofie? Does non-commitment Drake have a girlfriend?" She folded her arms over her full chest, pushing her tits up. This was not the way to be talking about the woman I longed for.

"Not exactly... but I... oh God... I love her..." Those words finally hit Laney and she moved off of my lap. I quickly pulled off the unused condom, yanked my pants up, and started putting on my shoes. "She left me... I'm trying to get her back. I'm such an asshole... I'm sorry, Laney."

"Don't worry about it, sweetheart. I knew it would happen one day. I thought it would be me that found someone, not you. At least I got off, sliding on your big, beautiful cock, one last time. Thanks for the orgasm. Go home, Drake. No harm. You didn't fuck me."

I may not have fucked her, but the guilt still hit me. Her words didn't convince me that I didn't do anything wrong. It definitely wasn't right. I had to get the hell out of there. I stood, kissed the top of Laney's head, and said, "I'm so sorry. Thanks for understanding." Not giving her a chance to respond, I made a beeline for her door. Exiting her building, I walked twenty blocks home, trying to clear my fucked up head. I cheated on Sofie. Not really, but close enough... too close. Would she think it was cheating?

Reaching my townhouse, I walked immediately into the master bath, stripped and washed my body vigorously. I was trying to scrub away the guilt... the remorse. I had *really* fucked up. Enough was enough. I needed to call to my LA friend, my travel agent... and Sofie. No more wasting time. It was time to make everything right. It was time to settle myself between two long, perfectly toned legs.

SPRINTED. THAT IS the best word to describe how I made my way through the LAX terminal. Reaching the baggage claim area, there she stood, *my* beautiful Sofie, in a form-fitting, jersey dress. My guess was—no panties beneath. *Yum* was the first thing that came to mind. With lustful eye contact, we rushed toward each other. Taking her into my arms, I crushed my mouth to hers. She felt amazing. She smelled incredible. She tasted perfect. I couldn't wait to devour the rest of her. Grabbing a couple bags, we made our way to Sofie's black Audi Q3. Opening the back of the SUV, thoughts of throwing down the rear folding seat filled my head. I could've fucked her right there in the parking structure. "How far away is your house?"

"Forget about it." She pointed to security cameras

and a guard traveling in a golf cart. Smiling, she turned giving me a little wiggle, then moved to the driver's side, and hopped in. Reluctantly, I walked around to the passenger side.

Watching Sofie drive, I couldn't keep my hands off of her. With my fingers, I lightly skimmed her body. Her arm. Her side. Her thigh. "I've missed you so much." Moving my hand back up, I tucked her hair behind her ear. I needed a better view of her beautiful face. "You're gorgeous, Sofie."

A smiled lit her face. "I missed you too, Drake." My heart raced. My pants tighten. My hands roamed between her legs. I was right, no panties. Very moist folds. "Stop... Oh God... You are going to cause us to crash."

"Then pull over somewhere. Anywhere. Now." Removing my fingers, I slipped them into my mouth. "Need to fill you." She laughed. "Please. Stop somewhere. Now."

She turned to me. "You're serious?"

"Dead serious." I leaned over, licked and bit her earlobe. "Next exit. Dark street. Parking lot. I don't care. Just pull over."

Just as I instructed, Sofie exited the highway, and drove into a residential area. She seemed as eager as I was. With the car in park, she immediately unbuckled, crawled out of her seat, lifted her dress, and straddled me. Rising up, I pulled my pants down my thighs, freeing my painfully-stiff cock. Thankfully, the car windows were tinted because I pulled the rest of her dress off along with my shirt. I needed to feel skin on skin. Capturing her mouth, our tongues danced. "Oh, Drake... I love..." Sofie moaned as my teeth grazed her neck. I wondered if she loved me or what I was doing. I hoped that it was that she loved me. I knew I loved her, but I wasn't ready to show my cards. I continued to play with her, grinding into her core, biting her nipples. Sofie busied herself licking and biting my neck. "More, Drake... more," she panted. Lifting her, I impaled her, enticing her to ride me as I bucked back, meeting her movement. Breathing hard, out of control, I reached between us, pinching her clit, driving us over the edge to our ultimate goal. Just as our breathing was returning to normal, wrapped in each other's arms... still happily connected, a car pulled up behind us with its high beams on. "Oh shit!" Sofie exclaimed hurrying back to her seat pulling her dress over her head. We laughed, relieved it was not the police. Making a U-turn, Sofie hopped back on the freeway and drove rather fast.

I've never been so happy to get out of a car. Her driving was fine, but I wanted to be connected with her again. I couldn't get enough of her. Jumping out of the car, we met at the back of the vehicle and I pushed into her, taking her mouth aggressively. She moaned, circling her hips into my hardness. Breaking our kiss, I hauled my luggage out of the back, and briskly moved toward her front porch. I needed to get her indoors or the neighbors were going to get a full view of me fucking her on the front lawn. Walking in her front door, I dropped my bags and quickly removed her clothing, then mine. Pressing Sofie up against the door, she climbed up my body, wrapped her legs around my waist, and I slid inside of her with a groan. For the next three days, we never left her house. Never got dressed. Never separate for more than a few minutes.

MONDAY AFTERNOON, I pried myself away from *my girl* to take a meeting with Dave. I wanted to have more time with Sofie. I needed his help. I knew Sofie's director friend, David Maxsam, a few years before she did. We met in a Pre-Production class I ended up in when one of my required art classes was not offered. Our teacher was a well-known romantic comedy film producer. His class was anything, but boring. It was a pleasure to attend. As an extra bonus, the class included a couple weekend seminars, in which, famous directors visited our classroom to share their film experiences with us. We listened to several humorous scenarios along with distressing issues letting us know shit happens. This was not an easy industry. Also, the reality was, in many instances, it was all about who you knew rather than what you knew. *Hang tough and never give up your dream* was the general message.

When our instructor announced a two-hour lunch break between speakers, the dude sitting next to me nudged my arm and asked if I wanted to grab some lunch. "Sounds good," I replied. Then looking more closely at him, I hoped he didn't think I was interested. He was fashionably dressed in designer jeans, white t-shirt, a button-down sweater vest with expensive Italian dress-shoes. Not to mention, he was so pretty. I wasn't sure. He had flawless skin, dark, perfectly-groomed hair and light amber eyes that were almost gold. I wasn't worried. I had a couple gay friends back in Boston and would have no problem setting him straight. Once seated in an upscale burger joint, I quickly found out he was very heterosexual when our extremely attractive waitress commented about his eyes. He was quick to pour on the charm, telling her they were *Oscar gold*. I laughed my ass off. "Laugh now, but someday . . . mark my word . . . I will be holding one of those shiny statues right next to my matching eyes." Damn, if he wasn't correct. He won one of those golden statues, and he was hoping for another with his upcoming film.

During lunch, I learned that Dave was from the East Coast like me. His grandfather was part Hollywood royalty and had enchanted him with stories. Knowing he wanted to be part of that world, he made Super8 movies with his neighborhood friends. Completing his first screenplay in high school, he started researching film schools. We met in his first year of college. He was taking this class hoping to make some connections to get his first student film underway. Yes, he could've gotten help from his family, but he wanted to gain notoriety on his own. He had a great concept for his first film. It interested me tremendously, and by the time we were heading back to class, he had finagled me into taking part in the production.

Over the next couple years, I worked on all of Dave's projects behind the scenes and in front of the camera. After that, I didn't see him for a long time until our paths crossed once again. With me back in LA, we were to discuss his latest project about to start filming. I needed to talk to him about Sofie and some ideas I had. It was time to reveal my plans. I hoped it didn't back fire.

Chapter Five

SOFIE

S INCE DRAKE ARRIVED, I had been treated to a heavenly view, each and every morning, as my eyelids blinked open. Sadly, this morning, I woke up to a cold, empty space to my left, making me wonder. *Had I been dreaming?* The smell of brewed coffee alerted me that he was, in fact, quite real. Sitting up in bed, I stretched my arms up to the ceiling, awakening my body. Throwing back the covers, I crawled out of bed, padded to the closet, grabbed for a certain silk robe, and slipped it around me.

Walking into my galley-style kitchen, my heart beat wildly, seeing *my* man, sitting at a table in the nook area, reading a newspaper. "Good morning, sleepy girl."

"Good morning," I said, passing him for a cup of joe.

"Don't you dare take another step!" I stopped, tilted my head in his direction with a puzzled look on my face. "Come give me a kiss." Flashing a smile, happy to do as he commanded, I walked over to him. Leaning down to plant a quick peck, I was quickly pulled on to his lap. I moaned as two lips claimed mine. Yes, I was fine with this action every morning. Breaking our kiss, he steadied me on my feet. "That's better," he said, slapping my backside as I headed to a dish cupboard.

Opening an overhead, teakwood cabinet door, I pulled down a turquoise, handle-less ceramic mug. Walking to the refrigerator, I removed a carton of creamer, emptied some in my cup, put it back, and poured myself some French press coffee. I took my first sip of the morning then returned to the nook, sitting next to *my* delicious man. He looked yummy, wearing faded-denims with a tight black t-shirt. Loved his bare feet.

"Reading anything interesting?" I curled my feet up under me.

"Not really." Folding the paper in half, he set it down then pointed to another section sitting next to me. "Hand me the car page there. I better rent a car while I'm here." We really hadn't talked about it, but now I was curious as to how long his visit would be... *forever* would work for me.

"You can use my SUV if you need to go someplace."

"Not sure that will work with your schedule."

"I have my pride and joy in the garage," I said with a grin.

"Oh? Please tell me it's not a motorcycle."

I laughed. "Nothing like that, but it's only made for two people."

"So, what do you have tucked away?" He furrowed his brow.

Smiling, I answered, "Carmen…"

He abruptly cut me off, shaking his head, "Wait! Your car has a name?"

"Yes." I laughed. "She is a 1971 black, convertible Karmann Ghia with tan interior and cloth-top."

"How long have you had her?"

"I got her when I was eighteen. My parent's owned an automotive junkyard. My dad was always picking up cars to restore. Unfortunately, most of the time, he kept them for only a short while. When a new find would come along; he was on to his next challenge. I watched my mother and especially my sister suffer the loss of cars they had grown attached to. He happened to get his hands on a BMW2002. My sister, Gracee, begged him for it. He gave into her. She had the car for two years when my father got an incredible offer he couldn't refuse. I watched her cry night after night even though he promised her another car. I never wanted to go through that. I think that's why I put off driving. Then one day, I was at the auto-yard when Carmen rolled off the back of a tow-truck. I instantly feel in love. I told my father I wanted her. He agreed to fix *her* up for me. Once *she* was completely redone, both inside and out, I made him sign *her* over to me with the understanding that he could never repossess her from me. She's mine for life!"

"Did Gracee get her dream car, too?"

"Yes, she did. She got a brand new convertible BMW. She wanted nothing to do with vintage cars again. To this day, she only leases cars. Always has to have a new one." I shook my head, thinking about Gracee.

"Does your father still restore cars for your mother?"

"No. They sold the business to our three male cousins. All involved in the car racing world; it was a perfect fit for them. They offered it to Gracee and me, but we both declined. With the proceeds, they retired to Florida."

"Do you see them often?"

"A couple times a year. Mainly holidays." Answering his questions, I realized this was the first time I had ever told him about my family. He had told me about his family, but for some reason we never got around to mine.

"Where does your sister live? Is she married?"

"Oh, hell no. No time for family. She's a career woman. My parents were hard workers. It rubbed off on my sister. She graduated from high school, bypassed college, and went straight into real estate. Gracee works and lives in Beverly Hills. I rarely see her, she's always traveling for her star clients, helping find them properties; residential and commercial. I can't imagine her settling down." I laughed at the thought of her tied down. "Ha! I have more of a chance at settling down with a husband and kids than she does."

Drake was quick to ask, "So, you do want to be married? Kids?"

Staring at me with his brilliant, lavender eyes, seemingly waiting for an answer, I felt a lump form in my throat. I wanted to reply, *yes, with you*, but since he wasn't proposing or offering to father my children, I had to keep it light... simple. "Someday." I didn't need to ask him the same question. He had told me on a few occasions, when we were around children, that he looked forward to having a family of his own. The subject had made me sad, it was time to change the course of our conversation. Lowering my eyes, I took a couple sips from my coffee cup. "I see you're already dressed. I better go get ready myself."

"What's on your agenda today?"

"I have to go meet my team this morning. We need to get schedules set up. It's really happening." A smile spread across my face.

"Excited?"

"Yes... except for the fact that I will also have to meet Mr. Model Maker."

"Maybe it won't be so bad. You might be pleasantly surprised."

I shrugged at his words. "Let's hope." Standing, I walked over to a copper farm-sink, placed my cup in it, then returned to the nook. Leaning over, I placed a chaste kiss on his lips then walked to my bathroom.

After taking a brisk shower, I pulled on a tank top, maxi skirt, sandals, and went to find Drake still in the kitchen. "What do you have planned for the day?" I asked.

"I have a few errands. Some important meetings."

"Will I see you later... maybe lunch... dinner?"

"Not sure. Let's play it by ear." I hated the short answers. *Why was he avoiding eye contact with me?*

I decided to put myself out there. "I'm going to miss you." Thankfully, that got him to lift his gaze.

"You will be on my mind all day." My heart thumped loudly in my ears. *Could he hear it too?*

"I rather be on you," I said, straddling his lap.

His strong hands promptly cupped my ass. "No panties. Sofie, put panties on!" I laughed, then captured his mouth, biting, and licking his lips.

Grinding my hips against his firm bulge, I encouraged him to connect us. Lifting up, he unzipped his pants, freeing his hard length. Grinning, I pulled skirt up around my waist then impaled myself on him with a moan. Leaning our foreheads together, we watched our bodies moving in a perfect rhythm. What a beautiful view; his cock slipping in and out of me. I hated when we finished. I loved the amazing orgasm. I hated the disconnect. I hated the goodbye kiss in the driveway even more.

Maneuvering my car out of the garage and down the driveway, I waved to Drake. My chest instantly tightened at the thought of leaving. I needed more time with him. I definitely wasn't ready to be separated. Truth be told, I never wanted to be apart again. *Get it together, Sofie, you have a big job starting today*, I silently told myself.

DRIVING THROUGH THE gates of a nearby studio, I parked next to a soundstage on the backlot, grabbed my handbag, and walked in to meet my crew. Introductions were made as everyone arrived. Listening to ideas and designs about everything from costumes to soundstage settings to location photos and more, I couldn't wait to get started. The morning passed rather quickly. It was already lunchtime. Damn! I hadn't called Drake. I hoped he was also busy, as I texted him to let him know lunch was out.

Just as I was having lunch delivered, David popped in. Kissing me on the cheek, he asked, "How's it going?"

"Pretty good. Everything looks great!" I was excited. I couldn't stop smiling. I pulled him around the space to get a closer look. "Let me introduce you to everyone. Check out their designs." Little by little, David made his way around the room, looking over designs, chatting a bit with each designer. Watching the interactions, out of the corner of my eye, I saw a man bringing in a couple of large leather portfolio cases. Then another man joined him as he began pulling out design boards. *Great*, the man who was assigned to my team. I sighed, then started to make my way across the room but stopped suddenly as the second man turned to face me. I smiled as Drake came into view. What the hell? I didn't tell him where I was going. Maybe David told him where to find me.

Walking toward him with a puzzled look on my face, I heard the man arranging the drawings address Drake. "Mr. Blaxton, here are your designs. The models will be delivered tomorrow to the studio." *What? What the hell?* I thought, looking between the two men, as I tried to get my head around what I was seeing... what I was hearing.

"Surprise!" David said over my shoulder. "Hope you like your new crew member. Don't worry, I'm going to waive my *no fraternizing policy* between employees."

"Ha! That's a laugh. This is a movie set. I doubt you can ever enforce that," I said still looking at *Mr. Model Maker.* I couldn't make myself move forward toward Drake. I was speechless. I didn't want to talk about this or to him. I was unsure about my feelings. I was confused. *Was I mad? Was I happy?* I wasn't sure. I had no choice in the matter. He was *handpicked.* I would have to make this work. This made me think about how I would move forward as if he was just another team player rather than my... *my what?* I thought he was only here for a few days... maybe a week. Not six months to a year for filming and post production.

David must've realized the tenseness I was feeling. He began to rub my shoulders as he guided me to Drake's work; design boards, blueprints, and a laptop, displaying various three-dimensional models. "Look at his work, Sof, it is brilliant."

He was right. The drawings were stunning. I knew he was talented, but these were amazing. He had stepped into a new realm, and succeeded. I didn't know how to communicate to him. All I could do was nod my head. I couldn't look at him. I didn't mean to be rude, but speaking to him wasn't an option at this point. I had so many questions. Instead, I addressed the team as a whole, said a few encouraging words, then spent the rest of the day acting as normal as possible.

AT THE END of the day, everyone packed up their items and said their goodbyes. Drake and I had not spoken more than what was necessary until we made our way to the parking lot. He walked along side of me to my car. It felt awkward. We had never had a situation like this. I didn't like it. We needed to get through this. We would get through it.

Reaching my car, I unlocked and opened the door, then tossed my bag across to the passenger seat before I turned to him. I was ready for answers. Leaning back against my car, I folded my arms, looking him directly in the face. "Why?"

Scrubbing his hands over his stubbled chin, locking his fingers together, pinching his lower lip with his index fingers, he looked intently at me for several seconds before speaking. "I wanted to be with you, Sofie. I volunteered when you were working in *our* library. You didn't take me seriously. Hell, I didn't take myself seriously, but I hated that you left. God, I missed you. I moped around. My father told me to step up my game. I called Dave asking him to help me out. He told me what I would need to do. Told me what to design. I worked like a mad man day and night. Emailed him files daily.

He passed them on to the producers. He said they were impressed; I was in. All that was left, was telling you. I prayed that you wouldn't be mad that I went behind your back. The night you texted me that you were too mad to talk, I thought, *God, help me, don't let this ruin things between us.* I had to move forward. I had to convince you, if need be. Bottom line, I did it to be with you, Sofie. I ached without you. I hate every part of Boston without you." I was stunned… shocked. I just stared at him. "Please say something," he said, reaching out his hands to my arms. His lavender eyes searched mine. *What were they looking for? Forgiveness… understanding?*

I should be thrilled he would do anything to be with me, but I knew they picked him first. They only wanted me… with him. "You had the gig before me. You would've worked with another designer."

"No. I told Dave I would only be willing to come on board if you were my boss. He said he loved your work. The producers loved your work. I was just another team member. He called me after he told you. He told me I needed to tell you. I should've told you. I was scared. I thought telling you in person would be better. Surprising you may not have been the right way, but I took a chance… Do you want to fire me, *boss*?"

I laughed, dropping my arms from my chest. "You like the idea of me being your boss… in charge of you?" I grinned up at him.

"On the set, yes. In all other areas, definitely not," he

said pulling me away from my car, into his arms. "Are we good?"

I wrapped my arms around his neck. "We're good," I answered before he crushed his mouth to mine, briefly.

Hugging me tight, he kissed my forehead. "Let's go home. I feel the need to dominate *my boss*."

Chapter Six

DRAKE

THANKFULLY, SOFIE TOOK to me being on her team better than I anticipated. I was happy everything was out in the open. I loved that she was conversing with me, even asking me questions about the project we were now submerged in daily. Her enthusiasm was infectious. Her visions for the film were incredible. She made working a pleasure . . . in more ways than one. Besides learning about her professional life, she was finally letting me in.

Day and night we were together; working and playing. Being on other side of the camera was fascinating... better than being filmed. It was amazing to watch how the animators and special effects team took my drawings, (both third-dimensional computer and one-dimensional hand renderings), along with my models, and put them into motion. But the greatest excitement of all for me, was in Sofie's face... her beautiful face. She was so passionate about every aspect of the designing process. She was so good with the team. Such a great listener. She knew just how to handle people. She was so diplomatic when she was less than thrilled with an opinion... an idea. It was bizarre to hear her talk about me and my work like we were nothing more than co-workers. I guess we were co-workers! However, when we were away from the crew, we were definitely more... much more. She was no longer the boss... definitely, not in control... not by a long shot.

I loved our daily routine. However, some mornings were painful; watching Sofie meditate and do yoga moves in her back garden while I ran on treadmill in her gym room. Some days, I could handle her downward dog, others, I abandoned running to join her in a series of our own creative poses. Our workouts were usually followed by showers, in which, we conserved water. There always seems to be a drought in California. We did our best to help the state. After clean-up time, we enjoyed a light breakfast and coffee. If we weren't on location, we often worked, at side-by-side drafting tables, in a studio in the back of Sofie's property. Yes, the tables were also convenient for *extracurricular activities*. Hard to be around *my girl* and not partake in her body. Lunchtime, we often packed our infamous picnic basket and headed for one of the many parks that were close to her house, or in the privacy of her backyard. That might have been my personal favorite locale. I think anyone could figure out *why*. If we had nothing crucial on our schedule, we made our way to Zuma Beach. Most nights we spent at home, grilling, and eating outdoors. Her jacuzzi surrounded by a teakwood-deck, which sat just to the side of her studio, was a nice way to relax and unwind after a long day.

One night, sitting in the spa, looking at house, I wondered why Sofie bought it. Taking a sip from my glass of Pinard Bordeaux, I commented with great apprehension, "This place doesn't reflect you... or your personality at all." I didn't want to insult her.

Fortunately, she laughed. "I know. Although, I do love many things about it. You're right, though. It seems lonely... foreign... resort-ish. It's not real. *Your* house is real. A real place to live... for a family. Mine is for a single person. I love your townhouse. It's warm. Inviting." She sighed, "Mine is impersonal... like a spa..." Her voice seemed sad. I didn't mean to make her sad.

When I first arrived at her house, I was surprised. I knew she lived in a California bungalow, but I envisioned it would be a cozy cottage, more craftsman-style than Balinese. Neutral colors flowed throughout with some chartreuse green and copper accents. All cabinetry was teakwood. Most of the furniture was made of bamboo. In her master bedroom, she had a dark wood, four-poster bed-frame, draped with white mosquito netting. Everything perfect for a tropical getaway. Nothing like the architecture she had told me that she adored.

"I like your home, Sofie... but I do love you in *our* home in Boston." She smiled, snuggled into me, and whispered, a "thank you," before climbing onto my lap.

Sofie riding me in the jacuzzi made me forget all about missing the season changes back home. If I was with her, I could endure the perpetual summer of California and enjoy our intimate life together outdoors.

However wonderful most of our time together was, there were also some unfortunate moments in our routine. Too many lately, where I had to share her. Tonight was one of those that I wasn't looking forward to; attending an industry party. After seeing what Sofie was wearing, I really didn't want to go. Sitting on the bed, slipping on my shoes, a lovely *vision in red* caught my eye. Painted red lips matched the slinky, body skimming fabric that enhanced every delicious curve. That dress was made to be ripped off—plain and simple. Watching her, my slacks were suddenly becoming extremely uncomfortable as she walked to me, ever so slowly. She knew the dress screamed, "Fuck me!" She was playing it up. I, however, knew how to put an end to her game which made us late to the event.

DRIVING UP A steep driveway in the Hollywood Hills, our driver deposited us on the doorstep of one of our film's producers. The money-contributor was happy with the way the production was moving along; on-time and on-budget. Opening his house for the evening, it was a *thank you* of sorts, along with a charity fundraiser. Seemed like every party these days had to be associated with an underlying cause. Besides the celebration, tonight, a new cinematographer was being introduced to the cast. Unfortunately, last week the original guy on the team had a heart attack. Thankfully, he did not die, but he was definitely out of commission for rest of the filming. There were a couple guys in the running. Tonight, we would all be privy to the big decision.

Entering the modern, glass house, we were greeted with a stunning panoramic view of city lights thanks to a crystal clear, star-filled night. I have to say I preferred the twinkling *stars* in the sky to the ones milling about the party; real ones and wannabes. Walking around, I remembered what I hated so much about the Hollywood crowd. In this town, I could count my real friends on one hand... maybe one and a half. We were surrounded by: the cut throats, the fakes, the greedy, the backstabbers, the whores (male and female); all in search of fame. I disliked these gatherings just as much, years ago, but I was here for Sofie. She had a leading role in the project. I would never leave her completely alone with these vultures. I looked forward to the moment she said, "It's a wrap."

In the meanwhile, we busied ourselves, sucking down free-flowing glasses of champagne and savoring some wonderful, hand-passed hors d'oeuvres while socializing. To be fair, I can't say that I despised everyone at the party. There were a few cast and crew members that I liked. I can say, I actually enjoyed the beginning of the evening. That is, up until the big announcement, and then the party took a big turn for me. Going from bad to worse. We couldn't leave fast enough.

It started with Dave tapping a piece of silverware to his champagne glass, drawing everyone's attention. The man of the hour; a scruffy, stubbled, pretty-boy-face guy with long, never-been brushed looking, dirty-blond hair walked up to stand beside Dave. He was dressed in baggy pants, short-sleeved button down Tommy Bahama style shirt, and flip flop sandals. You would swear he just stepped off the beach. *Beach bum* would best describe him. Looking closer, I then recognized him at once. Blaine Keegan. I hadn't seen him in years. I hoped he had changed... matured. I hoped the *asshole* was over his petty behavior. I didn't need shit with him, again. No history repeating itself, please! I wore a phony smile, like the rest of the crowd, as Dave pointed him in my direction.

"You remember Drake," I heard Dave say.

Reaching out, I shook his hand while my other arm remained tightly around *my* Sofie. "Yes, Blaine, how've you been?"

"Good... better now." I watched the way Blaine eyed *my girl* with his answer. I would have to keep an eye on him. Some people never changed. I was sure he was one of them. I was happy when Dave whisked him off in the opposite direction.

One shitty moment down, but it was quickly followed by another when one of the producers called to Sofie to join them. Placing a chaste kiss on my lips, promising to be right back, she strolled out of my grasp. Watching her smile as people were introduced to her brought a smile to my face. A warmth to my heart. I hoped she realized who was blowing sunshine up her ass… mmmm… *her fine ass*. Keeping an eye on her, I found myself swarmed by a couple, barely clothed, big-boobed starlets. They were incredibly gorgeous with their perfectly enhance bodies, but I preferred Sofie's *naturally* beautiful body. I loved all of her *real* parts. These women were looking for a meal ticket… a good time. You could spot them a mile away, it was as if neon lit signs pointed to them *groupies… casting couch cunts*. Not my cup of tea. Yes, I fucked one or two back in my early film days, before I knew better. I was young with a stiff cock that had no conscious; it pointed the way without regard to my head or heart. Now, my heart belonged to only Sofie. I needed to find her.

They were not giving up. They were coming on strong, pawing at me. "Sorry girls, not going to happen," I said to their suggested threesome offer.

"Well, maybe we will have a scene with you. We heard you will be acting in the film." I hadn't even agreed to the part offered to me. *How did they know?*

"Yeah, maybe we could add a sex scene," the other one said licking her lips. I just shook my head. I was *so* not interested.

"If you change your mind…" Stopping mid-sentence, she pointed a finger with a smirk on her heavily made-up face. "Oh, looks like your playmate is finding her own fun." I followed her extended, long nail to where Blaine had his hand on the small of Sofie's back.

"Definitely not," I said trying push away from the *double-trouble, plastic dolls* to get *my girl*, but I quickly lost sight of Sofie.

Looking for her, I became more aware of the sex and drugs available tonight, they were everywhere. I was sure that some of the scantily clad women, sashaying around, were on the payroll, ready to entertain at the wink of an eye. I also witnessed a multitude of sly hand exchanges to know; say the word and drugs could be placed in your palm. A little more discreet then the old days, but it was obvious they were present. I stuck with alcohol as my drug of choice.

"Hey you, I think you need some food," *my* beautiful Sofie whispered in my ear then followed up with a bite to my earlobe.

"I am hungry for you," I said taking her into my arms.

Her tongue licked up the side of my neck. "You taste pretty good." She sunk her teeth in.

"Oh God," I groaned, feeling the front of my pants tighten. "Be careful. I have no problem spreading you out on the buffet table and feasting."

"Mmmm... you do like to take me in public." She flashed me a sexy smile. "Did those very voluptuous women get you turned on?" God, *my* woman knew how to torture me, skimming her hand over my raging erection.

"They are not my flavor, but I was shocked that they knew about the possible role I may take." I steered Sofie out the open floor-to-ceiling glass doors to the backyard.

"You know this industry. Word travels fast. You are perfect for the character. You should do it. You will be every woman's flavor of choice." She grinned, licking her lips. "I find you delicious."

"Speaking of flavor… delicious…" I picked up the pace. She was killing me. Around the corner of the house, making our way to the edge of the property, we could see the LA skyline lit up in the distance. It always reminded me of the *Emerald City,* the way the buildings were clustered. Out of full view, from our fellow party goers, I pushed her up against a glass barrier, lifted her dress to her waist, and nuzzled her mound with my eager mouth. I wanted to strip her of her *evil dress*. I had to taste her. I could smell her arousal. It was driving me crazy.

Her fingers grasped my hair, she pushed into my lips, moaning, "Mmmm… I need more." I knew her well enough to know what she wanted. Slipping two fingers inside her slickness, I rubbed her velvety front wall, igniting a riot within her body.

Once the quaking subsided, I stood up and turned her around. "Hold on tight, Sofie. I'm going to fuck you hard and fast." Unzipping my pants, leaning over her body, tipping her head to the side, I captured her mouth with mine, and entered her swiftly to the hilt. Guttural sounds vibrated in our throats as we found our rhythm, climaxing one after the other. It wasn't enough. "Please tell me we can leave," I panted, reluctantly leaving her body.

"Yes…" she answered breathlessly as I adjusted her dress, which I would be deleting from her *public* wardrobe. I would do my best to keep others from mind fucking her… especially Blaine.

Chapter Seven

SOFIE

AFTER THE HOLLYWOOD party, production moved full speed ahead, and we were off on location. Drake agreed to play the part due to a lot of prodding from David. The schedule was worked out to allow for his dual-roles. I don't think he was very happy in front of the camera, but he was so good at it. Truly a natural. The camera loved him, while the cameraman appeared to have a completely opposite feel for him. I don't know what was between them. Obviously, something from their student film days. I didn't push. I didn't ask. Blaine seemed to rub him wrong. Even the mere mention of his name. I decided that when the time was right, he would tell me... or not. I would not be rocking the boat. All he told me was, "Please try to avoid being alone with him." I was fine with that. I had no desire to be alone with any man but *mine*.

Often, I kept feeling like I needed to pinch myself. I went to bed every night and woke up every morning with *my* beautiful, lavender-eyed man. I wasn't sure if it was healthy or dangerous for my heart to beat so rapidly all the time. I loved having him in my home and out on location. If not for the hours that we actually worked, it was like being on vacation. Our filming days were action-packed with long hours, but as long as we collapsed *together* at night; all was right in the world. I had Drake next to me. I loved everything about him...

His skin... firm but soft.

His scent... manly... musky.

His taste... yummy.

God, I loved him. My list could go on and on.

"What did you say, Sofie? Something about yum?" I heard a husky voice coming from the chaise next to me in our rented villa.

"What?" Opening my eyes, I turned my face toward *my* serious looking man. *What had I said?* I was thinking about how I loved being with him. *Did I actually say parts rather than think them? Was I talking to myself loudly?*

"Do you love me?" Oh, God. *How much did I verbalize? Could I back slide?* I just stared at him, biting my lower lip. "Stop biting your lip, Sofie. That's my lip to bite." He smiled. I smiled back. Yes, I was safe. I could change the subject or, better yet, silence any further uncomfortable conversation. I moved on to his lounge chair. "I know what you're doing. You are not going to get away with it." I snuggled up to him, nibbling his neck, hiding my face. "You can try to hide, but I still want an answer."

I breathed him in. "I'm not hiding." Reaching up, I

untied the strings of my top, letting the fabric fall away, exposing my pert nipples. I heard him groan. I was getting to him. I rubbed my lower anatomy up against the hard front of his shorts. I felt my bikini bottoms leave my body. Yes, I had escaped… or so I thought.

Flipping me on to my back, Drake's mouth moved over my body. Taking each hard nub into his mouth, he paid fabulous attention to both of them before moving on. Wandering hands and lips caressed every inch of my torso, trailing down between my legs. Settled in, two strong hands cradled my backside while his tongue and teeth teased my slick folds. I panted as a building sensation spread throughout my body. *Yes, just give me two fingers… inside… please,* I thought when I felt him shift. Vibrations were what hit me first, then I realized they were accompanied by his words. He was talking. He wasn't letting me get away with anything. "Do you love this?" I nodded. "I can't hear you. Say you love it."

I panted breathlessly as he continuously licked me, ever so slowly. Torturing me. "I love it, yes…" He graciously rewarded me with two fingers, I moaned. The fingers were too slow… too shallow… "more… more…" I begged in a whisper.

"More? You want more?"

I nodded.

"You love it?"

I nodded. The slight movement continued. He was killing me. He was holding out. I tried to move… on his face… on his fingers. I was dripping. "Oh so wet. I love it. You taste so good." He sucked on my clit hard. I began panting, "*Yes*."

"Yes? Yes, you love me, Sofie?"

"Yes..." I whispered as tears fell from my eyes. I did. I loved him. His hands left my body. I wanted to scream, "no," but then his whole naked body fell over me.

"Look at me, Sofie," he said wiping the moisture from my cheeks, while sliding inside of my body. Completely seated within me, I looked up into two darkened lavender eyes. Four words poured from his lips. Words I would remember and cherish forever. "I love you, Sofie."

I returned three of the words back to him before he crushed my mouth with his as he began to move. Satisfied with my answer, he gave me what I wanted. Rolling his hips, plunging hard... fast... building the friction, heating our loins... he took us to the point of no return... pure ecstasy like I had never known. Not even with him. *Was it the words? Was it expressing our love?* Whatever it was, I wanted more and more of it. I could never live without it.

THE MONTH ON location was eventful. I cherished our quiet moments alone in the villa. It was divine! I never tired of the *love exchange;* verbally and physically. If we could've avoided everyone at the end of the day, I'd say we were living in paradise. Unfortunately, the island where we were shooting was rather small, giving us limited options for lodging. Our cast and crew took over an entire resort. The chances of seeing one another were high, unless you were to stay in your room day and night. While we did spend a lot of our time privately—dining, drinking, and even dancing were fun resort amenities to take advantage of—here and there. Some people enjoyed what was offered more than others.

Leaving the calm, serenity of our villa one afternoon, we went for a refreshing dip in the resort's lagoon-style pool, featuring three swim-up bars. We were both thirsting for a tropical libation complete with a skewered-fruit umbrella. While Drake got us set up with a private, shaded cabana, I went to dangle my hot-pink painted tootsies in the sparkling, blue water. The party scene was in full motion; singles and not-so-single people, partaking in locale hook-ups. Typical for this crowd.

Surrounded by bathing beauties, spilling their good-ies for all to see, a loud Blaine was chatting away, copping some feels. Wanting to avoid him, I started for another area of the vast pool. "Where are you going, babe? Come join us. The more the merrier."

"Waiting for Drake. Thanks, anyway." I was on the move.

He moved quicker than I did, splashing me with a good amount of water, "Get in!"

Startled, I nearly fell in, but two strong hands cap-tured me. Familiar with that certain touch, I turned, smiling into lavender eyes. Saved again by *my man*... in more ways than one. "Let's get wet," he said scooping me up in his muscular arms, before jumping into the cool water.

Surfacing, Drake drew me into to him. Throwing my arms around his neck, I accepted his lips on my mine for a brief kiss. Feeling him hard against me, I moaned, wanting to wrap my legs around his waist. "Later... cocktail time," he grinned, pulling me toward one of the bars.

Lifting me up on one of the stools, he stood next to me, ordering our drinks. Yum; two piña coladas arrived in tall glasses with big hunks of pineapples attached, sporting cute paper umbrellas. Clinking glasses, about to take our first sips, *Blaine the pain* invaded us with his entourage. "Hey, man, put those drinks on my tab," he slurred loudly to the bartender. "They're partying with us." Then his arm was around Drake. He was right in his face. "Free drinks for my old buddy." Not wanting to encourage nor offend, we accepted our complimentary beverages.

Listening to a drunk man, bragging while pawing every female creature, was not my choice of entertainment. We attempted to converse quietly with one another to tune out our drink host. Unfortunately, he felt the need to invade our space, nudging Drake, trying to get him to contribute to his old film day stories. *My* man stayed calm, smiling, nodding, but not falling into Blaine's act-of-one. Once we drained our tropical treats, we ordered another one discretely then waded away with a wave to the remaining bar dwellers.

Exploring the watery surroundings, we found an intimate cove. Setting our drinks on the deck, Drake pushed me against the side of the pool. I latched onto his lower lip with my teeth, nibbling, and licking. The rum had gone straight to my head, my inhibitions vanished as I playfully hiked one leg up around his waist. Rocking my throbbing core into his hard length, I moaned against his lush mouth. Drake groaned, "Going to make you come." Standing still, he lifted me, giving me better access. Unabashedly, I moved and moved, building to a pending, much needed orgasm. Drake's mouth captured mine more aggressively, stilling screams that were sure to erupt. Right on the edge, one wave after another began to ripple inside of me when icy cold water suddenly blanketed us. "No fucking in the pool!" boomed above us. Jumping apart, we looked up to a smirking Blaine who tossed the ice bucket into the water. Then we watched him saunter off, laughing with three women hanging on him, in the direction of hotel rooms.

"Motherfucker!" Drake exclaimed. Tension plagued his face and body.

"Ignore him. He's not worth wasting your time and energy on. I have a better way for you to take out your frustrations. Take me back to the villa. Finish what you started." I leaned forward, up on my toes, bit his lower lip then followed it with a swipe of my tongue.

"Love to," he said climbing out of the pool, stalking toward our unused cabana. "I'll get our things. Be right back." By the time he returned, I was standing, waiting for him with a naughty grin on my face. Tossing me over his shoulder, he carried me to ecstasy. "You may not be able to walk for the rest of our stay. I'm keeping you naked and away from everyone." I was all for it. Grabbing his ass, he moved a little quicker.

For the rest of our downtime, Drake and I, as he promised, stuck to our secluded villa, along with the beach in front of it. However, for our last night on the island, David insisted on throwing a party in the resort's nightclub. We arrived late, after dining on the most incredible variety of shellfish . . . *my favorite*. Walking in, our eyes and ears had to adjust. The music was booming. It was dark. It was loud with chatter. It was packed. It was proving to be another drunken fest for Blaine. My whole body stiffened, I had had enough of his antics at the resort and on the set. I just wanted to turn around, to escape. "We won't stay long," I heard in my ear as Drake guided me into the mix. "Let's find David. Make our presence known. Dance a bit. Then take off." I nodded, letting him pull me through the crowd.

Sitting at the bar, we ordered a couple drinks since we didn't see David. I wondered if he set up the event for everyone to enjoy, but opted out for solitude. I knew he was overly tired when we met earlier in the day. Thankfully, Drake assured me if he didn't show within the next two hours, we would leave. Chatting away with our bartender and a couple crew members, the undesirable *Mr. Pain-in-the-ass* made his way over to us.

"Hey there! Well, if it isn't the public-fuckers." He laughed. Drake curled his hand into a fist. I rubbed his stiffened arm.

"Hey asshole... or should I call you ice-man?" Drake's voice was calm, though his body convened otherwise, as he put his arm around me. I could feel his tension.

Snickering, he pushed further. "Why don't you give her a break? Let her dance with me. Or are you afraid she'll see what a good dancer I am, and I'll steal her away?"

Before Drake could respond, I spoke up. "I don't want to dance with you, thank you for offering." I was firm, but polite.

"Your loss, babe." His voice was so cocky. I wanted to smack him. He was so fucking arrogant. Why couldn't he leave me alone? He was gorgeous with his messing, just-been-fucked, long, dirty-blond hair, piercing blue eyes, and a lean, sculpted body, but he was such a turn-off to me. Even if I wasn't with Drake, he would never appeal to me. Besides, I knew it wasn't truly *me* that he was after, he was just trying to get to *my* man. Fortunately, he gave up for the time being, walking away from us into a flock of women hungry for him. Something told me that would not be our last confrontation with *Blaine-the-pain*.

Chapter Eight

DRAKE

BACK HOME, I thought we would still be spending a lot of time together. I didn't think our days of being side-by-side would start dwindling. But lately, we each had more obligations. I now had two roles: actor and crew member. This morning I had to be at one of the sets earlier than I liked to deal with issues; technical model manipulations. Reluctantly, I left Sofie's warm body, took a shower, and got ready to leave. Placing a quickly kiss on her lovely lips, I said goodbye and walked out the door. Now, that we had to be at different locations, we often drove separately. I needed to go to several locations, and look at architectural elements before filming started. I could see that I would be spending far too much time away from *my* girl.

Early afternoon, I was overly happy to receive her text. Perfect timing, I had wrapped up my morning duties. I couldn't wait to see her.

"Finished our meeting. I had such a *hard* time concentrating… have you had a *hard* time concentrating today?"

"Someone feeling naughty? A wet panties kind of day? Oh, wait, you never wear them."

"I could use them today to stop the moisture from running down my legs."

"Mmmm… I will gladly clean you up when I see you."

"Hurry! Meet me in the trailer as soon as possible… I need you… badly!"

Thankfully, I had pulled over to text her. Especially, when she followed up her last text with pictures of her body… her naked body parts were plastered on my phone screen. Putting the phone down, I'm sure I broke a few laws, speeding to the studio lot. Once inside the gates, I parked in the first spot I could find, then sprinted to *my girl*.

Just as I was nearing the trailer, Blaine came walking out with smirk on his face that I would gladly have smacked off his pretty-boy-face.

"She's all yours now. Enjoy her while you can," he said brushing up against me as if there wasn't enough room for us to avoid each other. I heard him snicker as he strutted off. "Mark my word, Drake, you fucked with the wrong person. Enjoy your time in Northern California while I'm off with Sofie."

God, he was such an asshole. I wondered what the fuck was he up to. I knew Sofie loved me, but he was not to be trusted. *Was he still blaming me?*

I MET BLAINE Keegan when I worked on Dave's first student film project. He had dynamite camera skills. He and Dave worked magic. He took Dave's vision and brought it to life. He was so focus on set, but off camera he was an arrogant ass. A big time player; jumped from one chick to the next, or sometimes juggle a few at the same time. Another flaw in his character was his substance abuse. He especially wasn't great about handling his alcohol. Granted most people can't handle it after a certain point. He was beyond obnoxious when he drank and I have to say, I preferred him stoned, if he was to indulge. At least, he was mellow and quiet when under the influence of drugs. Hanging out with him, I quickly realized that I needed to keep my facilities about me if I wanted to survive a night out with *Blaine the insane* as he was labeled on more than one occasion.

Another thing I learned about Blaine very quickly, was that he could not be trusted. He loved competition and above all else, he loved to win, which meant he was a sore loser. He didn't care who he hurt, who got in the way, or how ethical or unethical his practice was to succeed. If by chance you did get in his way, watch out; he was not one to forgive. He was, however, one that was happy to get even. I learned this first hand as he thought I was to blame for one of his *biggest losses.*

I had been dating the daughter of a well-known Hollywood mogul. Little did I know, she was trying to capture Dave's undivided-attention. I was part of her ploy to make him jealous. He had known her for years.

Knew she was bad news, wanted nothing to do with her, and avoided her at all cost. When I caught wind of her motivates, I started backing off quietly. That was when Blaine started to move in. I didn't care, it made the break easier. I saw what he was up to, I'd seen him in action often enough. He didn't give a flying-fuck about her, but *her father* was a different story. He saw him as a gateway to the big time.

In the midst of their pairing... coupling... or whatever you want to call it, I learned more than I ever wanted to know about Blaine. I had always assumed he came from a Hollywood elite family, like Dave, but apparently he had made his own money. One night, Blaine pulled up in front of my Westwood condo in his red Ferrari 360 Modena and said he wanted to introduce me to one of his director friends. He had told me a few times, when he was out of his mind, that I could make *real* money . . . that he had connections. I should've paid more attention to his demeanor when he walked in to my place. I don't know why I didn't. Climbing into his car, he zoomed off, whisking us through Coldwater Canyon to *the Valley*. I saw there were cars everywhere as he drove down a long driveway to a ranch-style house. "Great. A party. Time to stay sober if I had any hope of getting us back home," I thought as I exited his car.

Walking in the front door, my eyes nearly jumped out of my head. There were naked girls all around. *Holy shit! What had I gotten myself into?* Music was blasting. Booze and drugs were being offered. I declined, while

Blaine indulged. Handing me a bottle of beer, which I nursed all night, he took me around to other parts of the house, introducing me to a couple people. Entering a big game room, he excused himself and wandered off. As I looked around the room, it finally hit me, I was in a fucking porn-house. There were explicit movie posters everywhere. When Blaine finally made his way back to me, he had a sleazy looking guy in tow. Introducing me to the guy as his *director friend,* I was struck again. He wanted me to star in one of his soft-porn flicks. Politely, I declined and reminded Blaine that we needed to meet up with Dave. The mention of his name had him in a panic and he agreed to leave.

Installed in the driver's seat of his Ferrari, I took us back to the other side of the Santa Monica Mountains while Blaine's story unraveled. As a teenager, he lived in a guesthouse with his single-mother on a property down the way from *the ranch* we had visited. One day, as he was making his way home from high school, a man approached, enticing him down the driveway. He had seen several voluptuous women coming and going on several occasions. Curiosity made him accept the invitation. With the promise of women, money, and sex, he fell into the scene. At first, he stood back, watched, taking it all in. Then he made a few suggestions. The director liked his ideas and put him behind the camera. Along the way, he had performed in a few flicks, but he was uncomfortable. Yes, he liked the sex part, but not to be filmed doing it. Proving to be a natural with the camera, he never stepped into a scenario again. Wanting to expand his camera work, he saved his money and enrolled in UCLA's Film Extension program, then met Dave through a campus bulletin board ad, "cinematographer wanted."

Reaching my condo, I offered my sofa to an inebriated Blaine to which he accepted. By the time I woke up the next morning, he was gone. I didn't see him for a few months until he showed up one afternoon and proceeded to punch me in the face, saying, "I trusted you." I figured it had something to do with our trip to the other side of the hill, but the fact that he had been exposed, wasn't by me. Once the story leaked, the mogul's daughter was quick to dump him. I never worked with Blaine again, until this project, simply because I left for Florence, Italy, and then moved on to architecture school when I returned. Dave worked with him one more time. Then, according to Dave, he took off to do camera work, internationally, until a couple years ago.

OPENING THE TRAILER door, I stepped inside, closed the door behind me, and locked it. I had plans for Sofie and wanted no interruptions. Turning around, I expected to see her in the lounge area or at least sitting at the dining table where her storyboards were spread out next to her laptop. Both areas were empty. Stepping further in the coach, I turned to a view that had me stumbling backward. Down the hallway, the bedroom door stood gaping wide open and there was she beautifully displayed. Lying on the bed, on her back, she had one arm above her head on the pillow and the other arm was resting over her eyes. She was completely naked with her ankles crossed, uncovered.

Looking at her, it hit me—that bastard got to see *all* of *my girl.* "What the fuck?!" I shouted, startling Sofie awake.

"What's wrong?" she said, sitting up and looking puzzled with wide, sleepy eyes.

Abruptly, I answered, "Blaine is what's wrong." Running my fingers through my hair, I paced at the foot of the bed.

"Blaine?" she answered in a questioning tone; confusion was written all over her face.

"He was just coming out of your trailer. Fuck!"

"Are you sure? I haven't seen him since lunch. We had a meeting in David's office. Then I walked back here. I texted you to meet me as soon as you could... a few pictures to entice you... I must've fallen asleep waiting for you." I loved the grin on her face. I hate that that asshole, most likely, saw her. I wasn't certain, but he'd have to be blind to miss that view.

"Fuck! That bastard wants you." I nearly pulled a hunk of my hair out.

"I never saw Blaine. I'm not interested in him," she said, moving to a sitting position with her knees beneath her amazing body.

"That fucker wants me to think something is going on between the two of you." I shook my head, trying to rid my mind of those thoughts. Thoughts that made me want to hurt him. I hated them working so closely together.

"Well, you know better... I only want you," she said, licking her lips, smiling at me. God, she was so beautiful, she made me instantly hard as I watched her get on her hands and knees. I groaned as she crawled toward me. "Mmmm..." she purred making her way to the end of the bed. "I've been waiting hungrily for you." Reaching me, she started undoing my pants. I pulled my shirt over my head. "I want this... only this." Moaning, she took my cock into her warm mouth. My pants fell to the floor. I stepped out of them. "Love your commando ways." She licked, nipped, and sucked me right to the edge, but I wanted her. I wanted to be inside of her more than I wanted to come in her mouth.

Pulling her up, she wrapped her legs around my waist. I could feel her moisture. "I love that you get so hot... so sopping wet from giving me pleasure."

"Then let me finish," she said in a whimper against my lips as I turned and pushed her up against the wall.

"Not a chance," I moaned, pounding into her wetness. She felt so good... so incredible as she sucked me in deeper. "This pussy of yours is always so greedy."

"It loves you," she panted.

"It's mine."

"Yes."

"You're mine. All mine."

"Yes… yes…"

"Say it, Sofie… Tell me. Who do you belong to?"

"I'm yours. Only yours."

Removing her back from the wall, I spun our entwined bodies to the bed. "I love you… oh, God… Sofie…" I emptied into her as she contracted and squeezed me perfectly. Rolling us to the side, we remained connected, wrapped around each other. Hearing her say, "I love you," as we fell asleep in each other's arms, made me smile. I wanted this *forever*.

Chapter Nine

SOFIE

I HATED LEAVING Drake behind. I was going to miss his warm, hot body wrapped around me. Unfortunately, it couldn't be helped. I needed to travel, since one of our scheduled locations had become unavailable. Of course, even if I was still in LA, Drake had to go up north to work with the special effects team. Either way, we were going to be separated. At least this gave me something to fill the time during the two weeks away from each other.

After two days of researching every nook and cranny available for filming, we were able to sit down to a relaxing dinner. The first few evenings, we were all exhausted, as well as frustrated at what we were finding. The original locale was perfect; this area would need tweaking. Today, things were looking up, and David insisted the three of us sit down to a good meal to celebrate a little bit of a breakthrough.

David arrived downstairs, in the hotel lobby, a little before I did. "Good timing," he said as he extended his arm to me. "I just spoke to the concierge. He assured me that the restaurant here was excellent. What do you say we give it go?" Sounded good to me. One less car ride was a big plus on my list after all the driving around we had been doing. "Let me just text Blaine where to meet us. He said he had some phone calls to make and would be a little late."

Walking into the bistro, I was impressed. It wasn't a typical hotel dining room. The decor was beautiful in shades of turquoise, lavender (which reminded me of Drake's eyes), and dark wood. The tables were outfitted with sofas, instead of chairs. It was inviting and comfortable. Seated, we looked over a delectable menu; the descriptions sounded wonderful. Matched with the smells, swirling around the room, my mouth was watering. I hoped the food was as delicious as the aroma.

Just as we had ordered our second round of libations along with our first appetizer, Blaine joined us. The conversation throughout appetizers and dinner consisted of how we could use each location to the maximum. It was agreed that we could photograph everything the next day and get photos emailed to different departments; let them get their creative minds reeling, as well. It took a team effort to pull it altogether. We were all thankful we had a good one. By the time dessert made an appearance on our table, David steered the conversation away from work. He took this opportunity to grill me about Drake. I gave him the basic rundown; things were wonderful between us.

"Glad it's all worked out for you, on the set and off. I

was afraid you were going to kill me. Going behind your back and securing Drake…"

"Good thing you hired me. Our friendship would've been dissolved permanently if he got the job and I didn't."

"I would never do that to you. Besides, he told me he wanted to work with you. He had no desire to work on this projection without you. I loved your work already. You were it for me. No doubts at all. Then I saw his drawings. I knew you two were perfect together… in more ways than one. Two of my favorite people, creating magic. What more could I ask for?" I smiled and was about to speak when abrupt movement captured our attention.

"Okay… I'm going to cut out," Blaine said as he pushed his chair back, tossed his napkin on the table, and stood up. "You two better not stay up too much longer. We have an early morning… need to see the location at sunrise."

"Thanks, Dad," David joked with a smirk on his face. Blaine gave him the finger and strode off. "Boy, has he ever changed. Not the flipping-off part, but he used to stay out all night, then get up at the crack of dawn and surf. He was the ultimate party dude."

"Really, he seems so serious all the time… around me anyway."

"I guess age will do that to you. We all grow up. I never thought it would happen to him, though," David said looking in the direction of Blaine's departure.

"Didn't Drake ever say anything about him?" he asked, turning his attention back to me.

"Nothing other than that he doesn't trust him. Also, that he better not touch me. I told him he has nothing to worry about." I took a last sip of my decaffeinated cafe latte then wiped my mouth while stifling a yawn. "I think Blaine may be right. I need to get to bed early. I want to talk to Drake, too. I haven't been able to reach him on his cell since we arrived. Have you heard from him?"

"No, I haven't. The special effects team probably has him working non-stop. I gave them a tight deadline. Blame me."

"Probably. I haven't gone this long without talking to him." I bit my lip, hoping nothing had happened to him.

"Damn, Sof! You've got it bad, my friend!" He laughed, signaling our server over to the table, asking for the check. "Go ahead. Get out of here. I'll take care of this. Tell lover boy *hello* from me."

Leaning over, I kissed his cheek, then got up to leave. "Will do. Thanks for dinner. See you in the morning. I will be the one propped up against a column, in the lobby, or lying on the floor." I laughed, walking out of the restaurant.

BACK IN MY room, I striped out of my clothes, slipped on

a t-shirt, and crawled into bed. Tucked between the covers, I plumped my pillows then I tried Drake's cell phone one more time before I went off to la-la-land. Just as before, it went straight to voicemail. Instead of leaving a message, I opted for sending him a text. "I miss you. I'm getting worried. This is so unlike you. I haven't heard from you in over two days. If I don't hear from you by tomorrow morning, I'm sending in the troops to find you." I decided to be funny rather than mad and demanding. He may be really busy. I knew there were some tight timelines, especially with him in the movie as well. Also, I didn't want to pressure him. But I was worried. One more text, "I love you," then I turned off the light and closed my eyes.

Awakened sometime during the night by Drake's custom chime, I scrambled for my phone. "Hey, baby. Miss you. Was looking at our film. Wanted to remind you. Hope it gets your pussy hot and bothered. I love you, babe." Hmmm... *baby* and *babe*, those were new. Film?

Clicking on the attachment, shadows of bodies appeared on the screen. As the camera moved in closer, it was obvious that two figures were female. Naked females. There was no sound. The picture was a little fuzzy. The women began touching each other, kissing. What was Drake doing recording a porn from his hotel room? What man didn't love to watch two girls? I started laughing... then I stopped. The camera seemed to jiggle as it pulled back to a wider shot. The women moved on to a bed as a male figure was entering the frame. Joining them on the bed, the women continued kissing over his erection, alternating in licks to him. Grabbing one of them, he pulled her to straddle his face while the other one took care of his genitals.

"Holy shit," I thought watching this... it was pretty hot. Setting the phone down, I pulled off my t-shirt, stroked my breasts with one hand and reached down between my legs with my other one to play with myself, I was so wet. God, how I missed Drake. Closing my eyes, I imagined him watching this, stroking himself, as a climax washed over me.

Opening my sleepy eyes, I lifted up the phone off the bed to turn off the video, and froze. Their positions had changed. So had the camera angle. It was a much clearer picture. They had switched around. One female was now lying at the end of the bed, and the man was fucking her while the other woman posed her bare mound above the other one's mouth. This was not being filmed from a TV screen. It was a film... a film of Drake and two women. The two women I saw draped over him at the party. The two women he was filming scenes with on the production, not sexually like this, but they were his co-stars.

Throwing my phone across the room, I punched my pillow then buried my face in it, sobbing. I guess, I had my answer why I had not heard from him. *While cat's away the mice will play*. My mother always told Gracee and me, "A stiff prick had no conscious." I guess she was right. I never imagined it would apply to Drake, but he did have a penis, after all. So why would he not be included in the generalization? Because he loved me. That should be the reason. Then I wondered, how long had this been going on? Since the party? Since they started filming? Since we started working apart? Questioning over and over, tears pouring down my face, exhaustion overtook me and I fell asleep.

Waking the next morning, I felt like shit; my eyes hurt and my body ached. I, unwillingly, got out of bed, and dragged myself into the bathroom to clean up. Out of the shower, I dressed, then grabbed my phone off the floor. I was surprised my phone had not shattered. Hiding my sore eyes behind sunglasses, I went to meet the guys. I was thrilled the weather was nice enough to provide me with a reason to don dark eyewear through-out the day. For lunch, we dined outside; another excuse to keep the glasses on. Some things were working in my favor. I was able to make it back to the hotel without giving away my state of being. Back in my room, minus my disguise, I called to David's room, making an excuse about cramps—my way out of dinner attendance. I let him know that I would meet them in the lobby the next morning.

About to take a relaxing bath, my phone sang *Boston;* Drake's ringtone. I instantly stilled, I couldn't move. Did I want to talk to him? What was there to say? He fucked up, sent me a film that was meant to be shared with one of his sluts. Did he realize his mistake? Now calling me to explain? The song stopped, only to start again and then again until it moved to his chime over and over. I could only imagine what his texts said. Then the hotel phone rang continuously.

Ignoring the non-stop noise, I went to run a bath to sooth my aching body and mind, when banging on my door started. Walking to the door, I looked out the peep hole; David. "Sof... Sof... open this fucking door before I have to get security!" I didn't want to open it, I just knew Drake had called him to check on me. I didn't want to talk to him. I didn't want him to see my puffy, red, swollen eyes.

"I'm okay, David. Tell Drake, I'm alive. I'm fine," I said with my head leaning on the door.

"Let me in. I know something is wrong, Sof." His voice was soft and soothing, but I didn't want to let him in my room or my misery.

"I'll call him right now. Don't worry. Everything is going to be okay. We'll talk in the morning."

"Are you sure you don't want to talk?"

"Positive. Thank you. Go enjoy your night, David." I moved away from the door as I heard him agree that he would see me in the morning.

Having no choice, I picked up my phone to call the *porn star*. Not *my* man. He answered on the first ring. "Sofie, are you okay? I've been so worried about you."

"Have you?" My tone was cool. I refused to rage.

"I just got your messages. I'm sorry, I didn't call you sooner. Work has been crazy. Wow! These guys put in tons of hours. I don't think I've logged this many hours in all the years I've been in employed."

"Long hours…"

"Sofie, you sound strange. Are you sure you are alright?"

"I'm tired. We've been working long hours, too. Nothing like *your hours of work*."

"I miss you so much. I tried to call you from one of the guy's phones, but it was like the phone gods have been against me."

"Why didn't you use your phone?"

"Oh… I left out that part. I lost my phone. I had to have a new one overnighted. It arrived last night, but it was too late to call you."

"Really? Well, you did call me." Hmmm… what was he going to say now?

"I haven't called you except tonight and then I couldn't reach you."

"Well, maybe you don't think you called *me*, but you did… I have the video to prove it."

"What video are you talking about? I didn't send you a video."

"No, I don't believe you meant to send *me* the video, *baby*… but you did, *babe*."

"Sofie, you are talking very strange. You're scaring me."

"Oh… well… let me scare you some more… hang on one minute." Hitting the multitasking button on my phone, I sent his text and video. Hearing the chime on my phone on his, I added, "Take a look at *your text*…

the one *you* sent me last night, *babe*."

"Why do you keep calling me 'babe'? Not that it is not a nice word. Not that I mind you calling me that, but it doesn't sound like you. You've never called me that before... and... and the tone of your voice is weird. Sofie, what's going on?"

"Look at the fucking text! *Look* at the fucking text!" I had lost it.

"Okay. Okay. Calm down. God, I wish I was there for you." He was quiet for a few moments. "This isn't my text, Sofie. It doesn't even sound like me. I see why you keep saying *babe* and *baby*." I was silent. "Sofie... are you still there?"

"I'm here. Play the video." I was cold. I was distant.

"Okay." More silence played between us. "I didn't send you a porn, Sofie. Come one. This is not from me."

"Keep watching. Better yet, fast forward it a bit. It gets rather interesting." Ice was flowing through my veins.

"What the fuck? What the fuck? This is not me, Sofie. I swear to God. I don't know what... oh, my fucking, God. That is not me. That. Is. Not. *Fucking*. Me."

"Be out of my house by the time I return. We have no reason to work together anymore. I will not be on the set when you are. When the film wraps, you will be going up North to finish special effects. Then you can go home to Boston. I have post-production to deal with. I don't need this... or you. If you wish to come to the premiere, stay the fuck away from me. I will have security. Also, I will be changing my phone number. Do not ask David for it."

"Sofie…"

"We are done. Over. Finished. You cannot explain this to me. You cannot deny it. It is right here on my *fucking* phone… *your* face is as clear as day… on fucking film."

I hung up… my phone did not ring.

END OF AWAKENING TO YOU, PART 2

Awakening

to You

FIFI FLOWERS

Champagne Girl Studio

Chapter One

DRAKE...

SINKING TO THE floor of my hotel room in Northern California, with my phone clutched in my hand, my chest tightened... ached. I almost forgot to breathe when gut-wrenching sobs hit my ears. "No..." echoed throughout my room, over and over. I wanted to call her back. I wanted to hop on a plane. I wanted to hold her. Reassure her. I would never . . . never cheat on my Sofie. I had to convince her... First, I had to convince myself.

How did this happen? What the fuck? There was no denying it. No mistaking it—it was my face. It was my body. It was fucking me. The picture was clear. I knew the women. They had suggested a threesome once, at a party, and twice, while working together on the set. Both of them spelled out things they would like to do with me... to me, trying to entice me. I said no, all three times. I had no desired to be with them. I loved Sofie. I told them it was never going to happen. The tape told a different tale.

I had never heard my girl so cold. She had made up her mind. She shut me out. It was crystal clear I needed proof, and I knew it. She would not accept my words. I couldn't just keep saying, "It wasn't me." I had never had sex with two women, ever. Yes, it was once a fantasy, like every other hot-blooded male has had, at one time in his life, but it never played out. Or did it? Was it me? Even I had to question myself. Yet, I had no recollection. Did they slip something into my drink? That would be the only way they could get me to do that to Sofie.

"God damn it!" I screamed, sending my new phone soaring across the room, crashing into several pieces as it hit the wall. I needed to see her. She needed to see the truth in my face. I hung my head in my hands, knowing she was gone for two weeks. I was stuck up north for at least another week. It was not possible to get to her.

Should I call her back?

Should I leave her alone?

The only clear answer was, best to leave her alone, until I knew where the film came from. I was pretty sure I knew who was behind it. I had to be certain. If I was correct, this time it would be me that showed everyone what he was really made of—I would expose him.

I began to question myself.

How was I going to get answers?

How was I going to get to the source?

How could I not get Dave involved?

How could I get a hold of the women in the film?

How?

How?

How?

That was the biggest question.

I needed help, but I realized it couldn't be Dave. I couldn't put him in the middle. He was her friend as well as mine. Then, there was Blaine, who I suspected, had a hand in my current dismal situation. He was also a major component in the film production. We all had to work together. I had no intention of causing problems during filming. Once Dave had returned from his location-scouting trip with Sofie, we got together, and I knew instantly, I needed to keep him out of our mess.

From our conversation over meat, potatoes, and a bottle of whiskey, it was quite obvious; Sofie had not fully confided in Dave. He knew that she was the one who had broken things off between us. I confirmed that it was one hundred percent her decision, but I wasn't ready to talk about all of the details which caused the separation. I did assure him that I wasn't going to give up. He was happy to hear that. He knew something big was going on; he told me Sofie didn't want to enlighten him. I'm pretty sure that was why he asked me out for dinner. I was under the impression that he wanted to see if he could patch things up for us. I wished it was that simple.

"Whatever is going on with you two, I'm glad you are willing to fix it. I will tell you what I told Sof, you two definitely belong together. I've never seen two people so right . . . besides Nelle and me…" He stopped mid-sentence to laugh and took a sip of his amber libation. "Let me tell you, we had our share of problems . . . but I knew she was the one."

I'm sure Dave never had sex tape problems. "Believe me. I'm working on it. I love Sofie. She needs to come back to me... I want her back now. Some things need to be worked out . . . solved. I'm going to do whatever it takes." I hesitated. I still didn't have a plan of attack. "I'm just not certain how..." I sliced into my perfectly cooked, medium rare, Kobe beef steak and took a bite, pausing my speech—my almost confession. I was afraid I was going to spill my woes. I needed to guide the conversation away from me. "So, what did you do to poor Nelle?"

"It wasn't me."

"That's what they all say," I retorted quickly. We both laughed.

Recovered from our snickering, Dave started his story of being an innocent bystander. "I swear, not me, at all. Believe it or not, our problem was crazy Mandi."

Nearly choking, I blurted, "That chick was mad about you. What the hell did she do? I can only imagine."

"You have no idea what she is capable of doing. She visited Nelle's salon to have her hair done. How Mandi found out where Nelle worked, or how she even knew about Nelle and me . . . I have no idea. Anyway, that crazy bitch went to get weekly treatments. She started confiding in Nelle, telling her that she was involved with a guy name David who worked in the movie industry, etc. etc. Every appointment, she fed Nelle tidbits about her relationship until Nelle figured out she was talking about me. Sofie had to come to bat for me. Nelle was already leery about dating anyone in the film industry, and had let me know, up front. The phone call I received from Nelle, when it finally dawned on her that she and Mandi were seeing the same guy, left me with my mouth hanging open. She basically told me, bluntly, with colorful words, she was not interested in dating a player. Me—a player? So not what I would call myself."

I laughed. Dave could be a flirt, but I had never known him to date more than one person at a time. He was Mr. Monogamous, but I had to rib him a bit. "Oh, come on; tell the truth . . . you had a stable of chicks."

"Seriously. When Sofie first tried to set us up, Nelle told her she saw enough cheating going on while she worked on various studio soundstages and film locations, before she opened her own salon. Sofie had to convince her I was different. Then, here comes crazy-ass Mandi, trying to fuck things up between us. Thankfully, Sofie proved to her that she was dishing her a bounty of bullshit; nothing but flat out lies. I was relieved when Nelle promptly canceled all of kooky Mandi's future appointments. She told her not to come back, then, alerted her staff that she was banned for life."

"Holy shit! That chick has always been bat-shit crazy. Great parents, though. What the hell happened to their daughter?" I continued to shake my head, shocked at how far Mandi would go. She would never have Dave. He had told her so many times. Yes, he had had to deal with a lot of shit with that one, but he had not actually done anything. It appeared that I, on other hand, had done a truly dirty deed that wouldn't be easily forgiven. "I wish our problem was that simple…" I bit my bottom lip to stop any possible chance of confessing.

"I understand. No more woman trouble talk. However, I don't think I have to tell you, but if you could keep it out of our work days…"

"Enough said. You have nothing to worry about. I would never do anything to sabotage the productivity on the film. We're all professionals. We will work through this." Raising my glass, Dave's joined mine in a toast. "To friendship…"

"And to the women that drive us to drink." Smirking at each, we drained our glasses.

The rest of the evening, shop talk ruled our conversation. A perfect distraction. No, Dave was not going to be my choice to ask for assistance. I did need someone that was in my corner. I needed someone in Sofie's corner. Someone who would be routing for us to get back together. Then it hit me—Sofie mentioned Lila would be our go between. Could I get her to help me? We both loved Sofie. She could be the one. I would have to put all my cards on the table to convince her as to how much I love Sofie, and that I would never willingly go against her—ever. Yes, it appeared Lila was my best bet, at this point.

TWO WEEKS LATER, production was back in full swing. I had arrived in town a week before and was still staying at Sofie's home; permission granted by her, through her assistant. Lila had come to the house, collecting clothes and toiletries for Sofie, who had other accommodations. I wanted to know where she was staying. I wanted to run to her, but I knew better—I needed to stay put. The house was mine until filming ended. I hated staying in her home. At the same time, it was the closest I could be to her without being with her.

Talk about being surrounded by her, there wasn't one corner that didn't scream her name. Of course, her cocoa butter smell was everywhere. I swear I heard her sexy whimpers at night, while slumbering in her bed; it wreaked havoc on my body. Thoughts of the last time we were together in her bed often invaded my dreams, causing me to wake up in a sweat. Reaching out to take her into my arms... to hold tight against my body. Reality always slapped me right up the side of my head. Wide awake, her face loomed in my brain. Her lovely green eyes captured mine, burning into my skin . . . my soul . . . my heart.

The day before our departure, I set about packing our bags for the two weeks we would be separated; I had insisted on being helpful. I pulled clothes out of the closet for both of us. Sofie stood back, arms folded across her ample breasts, shaking her head, grinning. I loved the beautiful smile that played on her kissable lips when she questioned me. "What are you putting in my suitcase?"

"Long pants and plenty of panties." I raised an eyebrow in her direction.

Laughing, Sofie walked up to me. Playfully rubbing up against me, she then climbed up on to the bed. Crawling on her hands and knees toward the middle with her skirt so short, I could see she was bare. Such a pretty view. She looked over her shoulder at me, smirking. "I don't like to wear panties."

My little vixen was enticing me with a little wiggle. Not one to disappoint, I moved swiftly to her. Pulling her hips back, I lowered myself to swipe my tongue along her moist folds, from her tight little nub to her wet, glistening, opening. Folding her head down on her crossed arm, she pushed back eagerly into my mouth, moaning, swirling her hips. She tasted so sweet. So utterly delicious. I tugged her right to the edge. Then kicking off my pants, I immersed myself into her tight, dripping wet passage. Nothing ever felt better than my girl.

We spent the rest of the day wrapped in each other's arms. Only breaking for food and to re-pack our luggage since our extracurricular activity sent the suitcases, crashing off of the bed, on to the floor. Waking early that next morning, I took in the exquisite sight and feel of the beauty next to me.

Her smooth skin lightly touching mine was so warm.

Her blonde hair was fanned out on her pillow.

Her dark-brown tinted eyelashes, resting on her cheek.

Her swollen lips were slightly parted.

Her breathing was shallow; I watched the rise and fall of her perfect breasts.

Thinking about those precious moments, lying alone in her bed, my body ached to inhabit her. My mouth watered at the thought of tasting her. To be in her home, surrounded by her aura, her aroma—it was killing me. I wanted to see her next to me, where she belonged. Unfortunately, I had to settle for seeing her at moments, when Lila informed me, I could sneak a peek. Sofie had made it difficult for me be near her, working out a schedule where she didn't need to be present. I owed her assistant big time for playing devil's advocate from here and there.

Those rare and wonderful moments close to Sofie, I treasured. However, on far too many occasions, when I did catch a glimpse of her, she was always around Blaine. I hated that Sofie was off with that certain cinematographer. I hated that they had to work so closely. I hated that my imagination ran wild when I saw him put his hands on her every moment he saw me near. Fucking Blaine! Her smiles, directed at him, made me crazy. Fucking Sofie! Was she leaning on him? Had she turned to him in the two weeks she was gone? Was he playing her? Or just me? I was jealous of any of her attention being given to him. She was mine. Was; the operative word. Seeing her with Blaine, had me feeling at an all-time low, until I heard her go off on him. "Get your fucking hands off of me! I don't know what your game is. Whatever your problem is with Drake, I won't be your fucking pawn. I'm not interested in you . . . never have been . . . never will be . . . fuck off!"

Her words lead me to believe maybe there was a light at the end of the tunnel. I just needed to get to the bottom of the sex tape scandal. The women would be on the set. I would talk to them, finally. Everything would be right . . . then my heart sunk a bit. "So, it is true, you're back to fucking Marco?"

"My social life is none of your fucking business. Why don't you stay out of it! You already ruined Drake and me, isn't that enough? I know you are not interested in me. You only touch me when he's around. Stop with your games. You won one little victory. Now, just leave me alone and crawl back under the rock you came from." Not giving him a chance to respond, she stormed off the set.

Marco? How did he know about Marco? Unless, it was true. Marco was back in the picture. It wasn't long after hearing Sofie's outburst that I started receiving photos of Sofie and Marco from an unknown caller ID, on my newest phone.

I didn't really believe Sofie would pick up where she left off with Marco. I knew she loved me. But it was obvious she turned to him for comfort. How long would it be before they got back to their old relationship? Time to move faster.

Chapter Two

SOFIE...

LOWERING MYSELF INTO a nice, warm bath in my hotel room, tears escaped as I wished the nightmare away. It had to be a bad dream, right? I wanted answers.

How?

When?

After I left?

A late night?

Was it not real?

Had I made a mistake?

He came home one night drunk, delivered by taxi. He said he was out with some crew members. Was that the time of his sex tape debauchery? Drake had told me, on more than one occasion, how much he hated the lying, the cheating, and the deception within the industry. How could he make these statements? Then do the same. It didn't make sense. None of it. He came to LA for me. He left his work, his home, his family, his friends—his life. He could hardly say that I didn't satisfy his needs. Since his arrival, we fucked like animals in heat. We never skipped a day. Often, more than once a day, we mated. Granted, I didn't bring another woman into our bed. Is that what he wanted? Was I not enough?

I wanted to go home. I wanted to curl up in a ball until the pain subsided. Would it ever go away? I had never felt this utter sadness . . . devastation . . . betrayal . . . love loss. I couldn't believe it. I was finally in love, for the first time in my life, at thirty-something. My first love. Now, my first heartbreak. Never again. I should've kept my heart guarded. I didn't need this. I had a job to complete. I had no choice but to stay. There was no escape. I had to soldier on.

After giving David a short explanation, stating Drake and I were over, I closed the discussion. Of course, he offered me a shoulder to cry on. I let him know that I did appreciate the offer, and when or if I was ready, I would take him up on it. I knew I never would. After all, David was Drake's friend first. Besides, I wasn't sure what to say. I had never had a situation with a man. Nor a relationship with a man. The only time we spoke about romance issues, they were about he's coupling with his wife, Danelle, whom everyone called Nelle. Since I introduced them, he had often confided in me. I freely gave him advice. How did I know how to give him advice? Common sense. Not reality. Not experience. Funny that I should suggest what he should do. I guess, maybe it was my own ideals . . . what I would want my man to do, if I had one.

Why had it taken so long to find a man or let one in? Why Drake? I had been with several men over the years.

Hmm, that sounded kind of slutty. However, it was true that I had experiences with men, but nothing more than a couple dates or casual sex. In high school, I was a bit of an artsy wallflower. I preferred hanging out in art museums and galleries. Boys didn't fancy art . . . nor did they fancy me. Fortunately, funky girl chic worked in college, making it easy for me to finally lose my virginity. Once I made my way in to the job force, I traveled often. I was always on the go. On the run . . . away from commitment. When I thought about it, it was unusual that I didn't strive for more. I was raised in a happy, loving environment. My parents were still married, just over thirty-five years. Yet, Gracee and I were still unwed and childless. Bizarre.

Speaking of my sister, Gracee, before heading back to LA, I contacted her. I needed a place to stay since I had already informed Lila to give Drake the go ahead to remain in residence until filming concluded. Gracee assured me I could say as long as I liked. She had no idea when she would return from San Francisco. "Sorry for being such a bad big sister, Sofapillow."

"You aren't bad. Believe me, I completely understand," I replied as she continued to explain her absence.

"My new client is proving to be such a challenge. He is not satisfied yet. Not that I'm complaining. He's gorgeous." I sighed a little louder than I meant to, causing her to apologize again. "Sorry. Last thing you want to hear about, is a man."

"It's okay. I'm happy you have found one that has

captured your attention. One that has you tied to one spot. That is amazing!" I laughed and she joined me.

"You have no idea, Sofapillow . . . no idea... But hey, enough about me, tell me exactly what's going on. I don't have a shoulder for you. I do have an ear that..." Muffled sounds drown out the rest of her sentence.

"Gracee. Sounds like you're busy. I'll be fine. Go. Thanks for the house. Please come home soon. I miss you."

"Sorry. Sorry. I'm the worst sister, but you're right, I have to go. I don't need to get in trouble," she said with a definite, strange giggle. "Love you." She clicked off before I could say goodbye. I hoped that she wasn't in over her head. In the same breath, I hoped that whomever was dragging her off, was someone fabulous. She deserved the best. I, on the other-hand, deserved a friend, at this moment. I had someone already in mind.

Marco. Yes, I requested his presence. I got lucky. He was on his way out West. His newest job was working as the stage manager for a musical, which had a six-week-run, at the beautiful Art Deco Pantages Theatre in Hollywood. Happily, he accepted my invitation to stay at Gracee's 1920s Mediterranean-style, mini-mansion in Beverly Hills with me. He proved to be just the right medicine for my ailing heart.

We shopped.

We dined.

We took in the theatre, both live and cinematic.

We floated in Gracee's heated pool.

We chatted about our romances. His new beginning. My failed ending.

He was one of my best friends. He was perfect for comforting me on my first breakup. He was a godsend on my days off.

BACK ON THE set or on location, I relied on Lila to keep the Drake path clear. I swear on a couple occasions she steered me directly toward stormy territory. Once, I nearly fell right into the arms of my ex-lover. A quick move, ensured my narrow escape of his strong hands, ones I longed to feel all over my body that tingled, whenever he was close by. Even minus the direct contact, the touch was there; his lavender eyes penetrated my soul, and I nearly stopped breathing. A lump formed in the back of my throat as I choked back a waterfall of tears that threatened to cascade at any moment. With one last glance, I clutched my chest to keep my heart from shattering, then walked away as fast I could. I ached every time I caught a glimpse of him.

Worse than being around Drake, were the times I had to deal with Blaine. Especially, when he saw Drake anywhere remotely near us. He would instantly move in closer. Corner me. Touch me, if he could. Those moments, he gave me the creeps. One day, I had had enough and I blew up in his face. My words seemed to roll off of him. They didn't faze him. He laughed at me, of course. I wanted to scream louder. He wanted to get to me. He wanted to get to both of us. I wanted to hurt him . . . slap him, and even more so when he mentioned Marco. He didn't know Marco. How could he know about my once-upon-a-time commingling with him?

I was confused. Turning to flee from Blaine, I saw that his sinister laughter was directed toward Drake, who looked hurt. His face displayed a sullen expression, his shoulders hunched. I wanted to say something. I wanted to explain. At least, he knew I wasn't interested in Blaine. Marco was a different story. Nothing was between us. Nothing ever would be again, but to Drake, I was sure he was reminded of the conflict with Marco in Boston. I wished, like last time, I could reassure him. That he could claim me like he did in the park . . . and on the set, after one episode, when Blaine was too close for comfort to me, according to Drake.

Late one night, as soon as the soundstage cleared out, Drake pushed me to a bed, on the set that was used for a shoot earlier in the day. His eyes were darkened. He wore a sexy smirk. He licked his lips before attacking my mouth. I moaned and bit his lower lip, stretching my fingers through his hair, he deepened our kiss. I wanted him to take me home. He wanted me right that minute. His fingers pulled at my clothing. "Not here, Drake," I panted. He didn't listen. "Let's go to the trailer." I tried to pull away. It was no use.

"I want you now." His hands grabbed my hair at the nape. He devoured my mouth. He really didn't need to convince me. He could have me anytime. Anywhere. Publicly. Privately. I was his. He didn't need to prove it, but I loved it when he did. For his benefit, I pretended to be against his PDAs.

Breaking our kiss, he continued his demands, "Here!" standing his ground. Gripping my waist tightly, his voice reminded me of when he fucked me in The Commons. He was jealous of Marco then . . . now, it was Blaine. The look on his face, the tone of his voice, had me soaking wet and throbbing for him. I would do whatever he wanted. It wasn't long before he let me know. "Now. Take off your clothes. Get on the bed. Spread your legs."

Backing up, out of his reach, I slowly removed my top over my head, revealing a pink demi-bra with black polka dots, paired with matching panties. I tried to be playful with a couple sexy dance moves. He wasn't playing. He quickly discarded his clothes, and then reached for me. He was so serious. A man on a mission. I was lifted on to the bed, my bra was unclasped, and my panties were ripped from my body. "For once, you wear panties," he snickered as he tossed the damaged scrap of fabric, pushing me on to my back. He then grasped my thighs, pulling me abruptly to the very edge of the bed. I knew this would be fast. I knew it would be rough. I knew he was claiming me, once again. As I expected, he took me in one swift move, all the way to the hilt, making me moan from the sheer pleasure of his length. He proceeded to pound my sex perfectly. I cried out as he hit all of the right spots while feasting on my breasts. Filled with his hardness over and over, slipping in and out of me . . . so good, he took us all the way home.

He always made me quiver with delight, no matter where we were. God, how I missed him. As I thought back on that night, when Drake reminded me that I was his, I realized he fucked me on the same bed he was fucking the two women. Holy shit, he had fucked them on the set, too . . . in the sex tape. Suddenly, that time entwined didn't feel so right . . . so special. It was no longer our magical moment . . . location. My stomach turned. How? How could he? I thought he loved me.

What was it with Hollywood? Did it change people? Did you get so wrapped up in the heat of the moment? The fake, fake moments of lust. That had to be what happened. People were only human. All day on a set, under cameras, surrounded by people directing every inch of your sexual moves. Yes, it was anything but sexy. Yet, let's face it, feeling a naked body up against yours has to cause some stir to one's libido. Many acted on those feelings. Many did not. I was sure that Drake would be one that would not. It looked like I was wrong.

Maybe I didn't really know him, after all. Perhaps he had acted this way in the past when he was acting. Was he showing his true colors? God, he so didn't appear that way to me. Was I trying to convince myself? Fooling myself? He seemed so sincere. Yet, how could I deny it? How could I look away from the facts when I had a full view shoved in my face? It was even worse, once I realized he claimed me on the very spot where he threw me away with his deceptive actions. Working on this set with Drake was getting more difficult. I was supposed to be enjoying my first time working on my dream job as a production designer. Not wishing it would hurry up and wrap.

Chapter Three

DRAKE...

NEARING THE END of filming, Dave insisted we make a trip up north, to meet with the special effects team. He wanted to have a look at their additions and to see if we needed more. Naturally, key players in the production would accompany us—Blaine and Sofie—along with a couple executive producers. A perk of having the finance guys on our journey; one of them arranged a private jet to fly all of us up. The down side, also the upside, of this ride was the closeness to Sofie. Near to me . . . and yet, so far.

On the day of our flight, we all met up at Van Nuys airport. Parking Sofie's SUV, I grabbed my overnight bag and headed for the tarmac. I stopped dead in my tracks as I saw Marco driving Carmen, Sofie's prized Karmann Ghia, with my girl in the passenger seat. Watching, she leaned over, kissed his cheek, then climbed out of the car with her bag in her hand and made her way to the plane. I was thankful the kiss was chaste. I couldn't handle seeing her passionately kiss another man—it would surely be the death of me. With the blood back in my legs, I followed her path to board the aircraft, but not before I heard the asshole speak. "Looks like someone's got a new playmate." It took every ounce of restraint to not stoop to his level and smash his smug-fucking-face. This would be a long weekend, sure to be filled with challenges:

Remain nonchalant.

Avoid killing Blaine.

Do not ravage my gorgeous Sofie, at least not physically. Mentally would be another thing.

If sitting so near to her in the cabin wasn't bad enough, staying in the same hotel, on the same floor, only a door away, definitely was. After check-in, we went up to our rooms to drop our bags, before heading out to the studio. Entering our rooms, I quickly noted that Dave and Blaine's rooms were nowhere near ours. I was starting to get the feeling that our mutual friend was trying to work some magic—shoving us together.

Dropping my bag on a couch in the sitting area, I received a couple of texts: One, from Dave giving us a departure time. The other one, a photograph of Sofie sprawled out half-naked on the bed in her trailer. The text was from an anonymous caller that continued to send me photos which stirred my emotions. Seeing this photo that was taken inside of her trailer, I was more convinced that Blaine was behind this buffet of images. Yes, he could've easily planted a wireless-camera, the day I saw him walking out of her trailer. I needed to let Sofie know her privacy had been invaded. Yet, for some sick reason, part of me loved all of the photos, except for the ones with Marco. This last picture had me stripping down for a much needed cold shower. I hoped it would help at the moment, but what was I going to do for the rest of the time she would be in my presence?

Refreshed, I changed into a new t-shirt then headed down to a waiting car Dave had hired. Opening the door, Sofie was already tucked in, alone. I stood looking at her. God, she was so beautiful with her long blonde hair, pulled up into a high ponytail. I longed to sink my teeth into the smooth skin on her perfectly exposed neck. Her dazzling green eyes pierced my heart. They spoke of love and sadness, all at once. Breaking our gaze, she looked forward. "Get in. Dave and Blaine hitched a ride with the other two, earlier." Just as I had thought, our friend was intervening on our behalf. Following her instruction, I climbed in, wanting to slide across the seat, and pull her into my lap. Knowing if things were different, the privacy window would be up, and she would be happily straddling me. I laughed silently, adjusting my snug fitting jeans, once again.

Fortunately, the silent car ride was moderately short. I did like that I had her undivided attention, even though I couldn't act on any of my thoughts. I wanted to say so many things. I wanted to do so many things to her. If only I could hold her tightly in my arms. Kiss her. Breathe her in. But all I had to do was look at her. Her body language told me; the time wasn't right. She sat rigidly on her side of the luxurious bench seat, her head was down, focused on her cellphone screen as she texted away. Defeated, I leaned my head back, closing my eyes. I must've dozed off because next thing I knew, a gentle hand was patting my bicep, accompanied by a lovely voice softly speaking my name. "Drake... Drake... Wake up... We're here."

"Sofie," I muttered, opening my eyes to see her curvy backside as she exited the car. Climbing out of the vehicle, I met her on the sidewalk outside of the facility.

As if speaking to tour director, she asked, "Which way?"

I wished to offer up my arm to her, but as that was not an option. I gestured with my hand toward the building directly in front of us. "Right this way." Beginning to walk, she followed slightly behind me, off to my right side. Once inside, we were greeted by a couple of the guys I had met and worked with a month or so ago. I introduced them to Sofie and they began to fill her in on things they were working on while pointing out departments within the studio. Her own private tour. I loved the look on her face. It seemed to shine as she took in all of the sights and sounds.

Finally reaching the rest of our group, we were escorted inside of a large soundstage, and then into an in-house screening room. Several questions were asked and answered after we watched the scenes unfold. They had done a truly amazing job with what they pieced together; real footage with magical creation. It was a remarkably flawless combination. The special effects were outstanding! I couldn't tell which were my models and which were the actual structures. Blaine's camera work was dynamic. As much as he annoyed me, I couldn't deny he was a brilliant cinematographer. Then it hit. Got me thinking about photography and how it could be manipulated. Was the sex tape another creation of his? He had filmed many of them. In his earlier days, he even edited them. Did he, perhaps, edit the tape?

I was lost in my thoughts when I heard my name spoken by those two lush lips I loved so much. "Drake... Drake..." There was no touch this time, but the voice caused my pants to tighten. It had been far too long since she was under me . . . over me. I heard myself groan. I hoped no one else heard me besides Sofie, whose eyes widen, telling me she was privy to my guttural noise. A second groan threatened to escape as I watched her bite her bottom lip. It should've been my teeth doing the nibbling. We held eye contact. I hope she realized I was silently begging her to believe in me . . . to forgive me. The longer we gazed at each other, I wondered what she would've done if I had touched her. A touch—that would never be enough—I wanted to devour her. If only we were alone.

"Excuse me, you two, but we have dinner reservations, tonight. I'd like to go back to the hotel to freshen up and change clothes . . . maybe rest awhile. We only have one car waiting for us at the moment, so let's get going." Dave's words shattered the illusion, or I should say, my delusional thoughts. As quickly as I hoped I had a chance, Sofie's wall was back up. Arriving in front of a waiting, black Suburban outside, she promptly hopped up in to the front passenger seat, away from me, while the rest of us climbed in the back.

LATER THAT NIGHT, we met in the lobby lounge for a cocktail before heading out to an award winning restaurant in Sausalito that was partly owned by one of the producers, whom was not present on the trip. Sitting on a leather couch, facing the bar entrance, I saw Sofie stroll in. She was stunning, as always, wearing a fitted, short sleeve, low-scoop neck, knee-length, pale grey dress with silver, and high-heel sandals. Every curve was on full display. No panty lines. I took a deep breath, followed by a big gulp from my crystal tumbler filled with two-fingers of whiskey, envisioning the pretty, pink flower with soft, lickable petals, beneath her garment.

She refused to make eye contact with me. "Are we ready to go, gentlemen?" They all nodded their heads, finished their drinks, and stood up. Sofie had all of us under her magical spell, even Dave. I had to shake my head and laugh. God, I loved her.

Once at the restaurant, we were directed to a semi-private room, off to the side, facing out onto the bay. An elegant table was set up for us. Glasses, along with decanters, filled with red wine from the producer's Napa vineyard were ready to be enjoyed. It was amusing to watch Dave maneuver us around so he that he had Sofie seated at the head of the table, next to me. He actually had a gleam in his eye as he looked between us. She, on the other hand, appeared tense, wearing a fake smile. I wasn't sure whether I should've kissed Dave, or punched him.

Throughout several courses of delectable food, paired with incredible bottles of wine, the main topic of discussion centered on the film. They were all elated by how well every aspect of the post-production was coming together. The anticipation of the box office. What the critiques would think. More important to Dave, what the academy would think. He was going for gold . . . gold statues, at that. Seated next to Sofie, I was privy to her movement when each new element was introduced. I soon realized, there were many instances in which Dave, unknowingly, left Sofie out of the conversation. Things that he should've asked her, he directed toward me. When he was looking for an opinion here and there, he never opted for hers. Yes, I watched how her whole body stiffened. Her hands moved to her lap, clenching and unclenching. I had a clear shot of her suffering. I hoped she understood, when I interjected on her behalf, as Dave asked another undirected-to-Sofie question.

"Dave, I think Sofie has some input on the overall concept. I think you might want to hear how she feels…"

Before Dave said another word the rest of the night, he was careful to include his Sof. I nearly came in my pants, when I felt her hand on my thigh. I turned to her with longing in my eyes . . . like a puppy dog, thankful his master had rewarded him with a bone. She mouthed, "Thank you," as her warm grip departed my leg. My body . . . my heart couldn't take anymore; I was so ready to call it a night. However, Blaine insisted on moving to the bar area of the restaurant for one more drink before the two producers headed for the airport to make their way home.

Reluctantly, I meandered behind them, to the bar, as Dave had helped Sofie up from the table. Curling her arm around his, I heard him apologize to her quietly as she leaned her head on his bicep. I wanted to trade places with him. Instead, I joined in with the drunken conversation as we sat around a couple cocktail tables pushed together and ordered, yet, another round of drinks. This time, I asked for something a little stronger. I'd rather be oblivious to my surroundings than endure anymore. The night was proving to be excruciatingly painful. It reminded being of the days I spent at the Frog Pond a year ago; watching her, wanting her, not being able to grasp her, hold her. Only this time, looking at the most beautiful sight imaginable was far worse—I had had a taste of her. I truly knew exactly what a treasure I was missing.

Then, just when I thought the evening couldn't possibly be any more unbearable, a text was delivered to my cellphone. A series of cozy photos featuring my Sofie and Marco. I scrolled through; some they were out somewhere eating, others, they were walking arm-in-arm. But the one that hit me hardest was of them lying next to each other on the bed in her trailer, parked at the studio. Once our refuge. She was now sharing it with another. Thank God she had clothes on; unlike the last photo I received earlier in the day. Though it still didn't matter, clothed or not clothed, I was worried.

What was she doing with him?

Had she turned to him again?

Were they just friends?

Had they become lovers again?

They looked happy—too happy. They looked like they were laughing. I hated it. I couldn't contain myself. "Are you punishing me, Sofie?" I asked softly, turning my cellphone screen to her beautiful green eyes that instantly widened.

"It's not what it looks like. There is nothing going on." She grabbed the phone from me. "What the... Where did you get that? Are you spying on me?"

"No, I am not spying on you. And... I could say the same thing about my situation. It's not true."

Ignoring me, she asked, "Did you install a camera in my trailer?" This question struck me. I was right, Blaine was behind this. The day he was in the trailer or on another occasion, he must've installed a camera. Looking around, where was he now? Off hiding in the restaurant, sending me these photos; films to Sofie? Shit! What other films . . . photos did he have of Sofie . . . of us?

"Sofie, I did not snap all of these photos..."

"All? What do you mean all?" I could hear an uneasiness rise in her voice.

"Someone is sending me random photos of you and Marco." Sliding my finger across my phone pad, I located my photo folder, and opened it to reveal several photos. "Take a look." I handed her my phone.

Watching her scroll through the photos, out of the corner of my eye I saw Blaine saunter in. He looked at the both of us. More importantly, he saw the look on Sofie's face. I wanted so badly to get up and beat the living shit out of him. Instead, I gave him the death stare—the evil eye. He was gazing intently at me. I'm not sure what his expression meant. There was no smirk. There was no puffed out chest. There was no triumphant gleam. If I didn't know better, I would've said remorse had taken over his whole face and body. So caught up in Blaine, I had not even realized that Sofie had vacated her chair.

Searching the restaurant, she was nowhere to be found.

Chapter Four

SOFIE...

RETURNING FROM MY trip earlier than planned, I was so happy to find Marco and Gracee waiting for me at Burbank airport. Funny, I had thought to call her on her cellphone to come rescue me, thinking she was still across the bay in San Francisco. Then, as I walked out of the restaurant, a couple was being dropped off by a taxi. Perfect. I asked him to take me to the airport. At first he flat out refused, but with the offer of a hundred dollar tip, he pulled away from the curb with me inside. Funny how money often gets people moving in the direction you desire. My luck may have sucked at dinner, but between the cab ride, catching the last plane out, and having two important people greeting me—maybe someone was watching over me, after all.

I rushed into Gracee's arms. I don't think I've ever been so happy to see her in all of my life. I couldn't help myself, tears poured down my cheeks as garble spewed from my lips.

"Oh my God, what must I look like to those producers—I just ran out!" That seemed to be my biggest concern. "Please let them be so inebriated, that they didn't notice." Then my favorite term rumbled and grumbled from my lips. "Damn boys-club!"

Gracee just held on to me tightly, stroking my hair, over and over. Reassuring me and telling me, "oh, honey, who gives a fuck?!" and "oh, fuck them!" to anything and everything I said.

Finally, there was a big throaty clearing noise. "Hey girls, let's get out of here. Lots and lots of cocktails await us at home," Marco said putting his arms around both of us. Nodding our heads, we all split apart and made our way to Gracee's newest BMW 7-series, this one was midnight-blue. With Marco behind the wheel, we made it to Gray's (Marco's pet name for her) sectional sofa, in record time. Outfitted in comfy clothes, we curled up with a large pitcher of martinis that had my mouth running away with details. This time they were not mainly about work, but Drake . . . private detective Drake.

"There I sat, at a table filled with men. First, as I said, they ignore me. Then they didn't. Thanks to Drake. And . . . and then, my knight in shining armor, once again, dulled." I stopped to down my glass, wipe my tears, and then extended my glass. "Fill me up!" I cried, literally.

"What did that bastard do?" Gracee tipped back her glass too. "Fill!"

Marco laughed. "Shit! If you can't beat, join 'em. I need to make more." After pouring liquid in all three, he was up at the bar, mixing a new batch. "Go on or I will not share. You share; I share."

That caused us to giggle, giving me time to regroup. "Where was I? Oh, yes. Marco, you and I have been under surveillance..."

"What?!" he exclaimed.

"Yep. Drake has had someone following me. Of course, you have been with me a lot. Drake had photographs. Several! Even ones in my trailer. Us in bed."

"How? Why?"

"He claims someone has been texting them to him. He said he did not take them or hire someone. Why would someone send him pictures of us? I think it makes more sense that he would have someone follow me... I don't know. He was jealous of you before..."

"Well he has no reason to be now."

"I know that . . . you know that—Drake doesn't. Blaine mentioned you in front of him a few weeks ago..."

"Who is Blaine?" Gracee interrupted.

"Some asshole; great cinematographer, but big asshole. He has it out for Drake."

"Why?" Gracee's inquiring mind wanted to know. Hell, I wanted to know.

"I don't know. I just know Drake told me to stay away from him. The guy gave me the creeps from day one. I finally think I got his attention when I yelled at him to fuck off. He's not my problem. There's more shit going on. Drake thinks I'm fucking Marco again. He doesn't know that you and Kimee are an item. Thank goodness Kimee was understanding of you hanging out with me."

"Who is Kimee?" Gracee was way out of the loop.

Kimee, the buxom waitress he met in Boston, had proved to be more than a bimbo. She was actually a college student by day, majoring in finance. The island-beauty came to the states from St. Thomas with her family when she was sixteen, ten years ago. Though she came from a very prominent family, she insisted on working as a cocktail waitress a few nights a week for extra cash. According to Marco, she liked to play the dumb card—it got her more tips. Until she was certain a man could look beyond her double-Ds, she didn't show them that she harbored a brain. Where I was concerned, she was a bit jealous in the beginning, but as soon as Marco started living with her, when he was not out of town doing theatre, their relationship had changed dramatically. I was shocked when he told me he was making every effort to line up work in NYC or Boston only. He had been avoiding the West Coast, until I called, and a job offer came through at almost the same time. Since he arrived, he called her daily. I even spoke with her a few times, when they video chatted. It was nice that he finally found someone.

After Marco was done telling us about his love life, Gracee hinted that her client had turned into so much more, but she couldn't divulge any details. I hoped he wasn't married. I wanted her to find the one, too.

Drunk me let them know how I felt . . . and a bit too much. "I'm so happy for you guys... I was happy until Porn Star Drake appeared."

"I thought he was Detective Drake?" Marco questioned.

"Now, he's Porn Star Drake? Spill the beans, Sofapillow, do not keep your sister in the dark!"

"Or me!" Marco exclaimed, and I unraveled the story to both of them.

"I find it hard to believe that Drake would do that to you. He loves you. I saw it that night in Boston. Again, Kimee and I are truly sorry for our behavior."

I punched him. "Ouch! I said I was sorry," Marco winced, causing me to laugh before tears sprang from my eyes. Putting his arms around me, he whispered, "Sorry, Sofa," while Gracee rubbed me feet.

"Where is this tape? You still have it?" Gracee asked.

"Yes. On my phone."

"Give me your phone." Marco stood up. "Gracee, do you have cables to connect your phone to your big screen? We need to get a better look at it this."

"I do, in the cabinet below the TV. Oh, goody, porn!" she cheered. I kicked at her. "Sorry, I forgot."

With my phone hooked up, via Bluetooth technology, there it all was. I found it difficult to watch. I turned my attention to my martini. Ugh! Just what I didn't need, Drake and the sluts up close and personal.

"Those are some nice, big . . . nice looking women...

Hard to see the guy…" Gracee announced.

"Oh, you will get a better view. Guess the cameraman hadn't figure out how bad the picture quality was until half through… Oh, here it comes…" I turned away and bit my lip, trying to stop tears from flowing.

"Holy shit!" Marco shouted. I knew he saw Drake's face.

"He's hot, Sofapillow!" Gracee equipped. Then I heard him start to laugh and my sister joined him.

I grabbed little throw pillows on the couch and tossed them at both of them. "My heart is breaking and you two are fucking laughing. What is wrong with you?"

"Sofa, do you recognize the room?"

"Yes, it's part of the set."

My sister laughed even harder. "Notice anything else?"

"No. Besides that that is definitely Drake; his face . . . his. . . . his body."

"Ever fuck on that bed?" Marco cocked his head sideways, gazing at me.

"On the set? You said he like public sex. The thrilled of being caught . . . watched…" Gracee said, staring at me with her arm across her body, her elbow perched on it and her chin resting on her hand.

"Once. Drake felt the need to claim me . . . to mark me, again." I sighed.

"I like him!" Gracee announced.

"Yeah, love how he's always pissing on his territory!" Marco said laughing.

"You would." I smacked him again with another pillow.

"Sofapillow, seriously, honey, you need to look at the scene again. Marco, rewind it."

"I've seen enough, thank you. I'd prefer not to keep watching it"

"I don't think you have seen enough," Marco said while playing with my phone.

"Start from the beginning." Here come the two girls. "You know them?"

"Yes, they work on the film." He fast forwards to the guy entering.

"Does that look like Drake? I'm thinking that that is not him. I think the picture quality is on purpose," Marco says.

"Okay, well when you fast forward, that is definitely him!"

"Let's move on to that clear picture, Marco." Bam! There he was and up popped my sister running to the screen. "Now look right here!"

Shit! I didn't want to look.

"Look, damn it!" Marco shouted, pausing the frame.

"Look right here!" Gracee pointed to the body of the woman Drake was fucking. "What do you see on her hip?"

Marco nudged me. "What do you see, Sofa?"

"What the... What the fuck?" Started shaking my head. "I have never had a chick sitting on my face!"

"But you do have that heart shaped birthmark; same

place I have mine." Gracee pulled down her yoga paints to show hers off.

"Yes," I said. Getting up, I looked more closely at the screen.

"Sofa, you work in the film industry. Someone filmed you and Drake having sex and doctored the tape. I'll bet money that that first part is not Drake."

"Who? Why? That's a better question—shit! Blaine!" The questions and answer rolled out of my mouth.

"What is the story between Drake and Blaine? Fight over a woman?"

"I don't know, but I've made a huge mistake—I've gotta go!"

"You can't go anywhere. You've had too much to drink," Gracee stated with her hands on her hips, followed by a hiccup or two. "Besides, he's not home. You left him up North, remember?"

"Well, that's true and not true," Marco said, dangling my phone in his hand.

"What do you mean?" I asked, raising one eyebrow at him. His voice sounded like he was up to something. He knew something else that I didn't. "Don't play games, Marco. I know you too well."

"David has been texting you." Gracee spurted out.

"You knew too?" I gave her the pouty little sister look.

"Don't do that! You know I hate it! We didn't know what he wanted. We didn't want to upset you. Marco looked when you went to change clothes, when we first got here. He told him you were okay. That you flew home. So they grabbed your stuff from the hotel and they all flew back down."

"He's home, Sofa." Marco said quietly and I started to cry.

"I have to go to him... Please... Please... Call me a cab, or I'm going if I have to walk," I said slipping on a pair of ballet slippers, wiping tears.

"I'm on it!" Marco used my phone to find me a ride over the hill. "Ten minutes..."

"And she'll be off to make a new porno!" Gracee chimed in. Shaking my head at Gracee's remark, we all laughed and they cracked jokes until the taxi arrived.

❦

PULLING UP MY driveway, I saw the Audi was sitting in there. I thought, oh, thank God, he really is home! Quickly paying the fare, I jumped out of car and ran to the front door. Unlocking the door to my darkened house, I moved through every room, searching for Drake. It was late, I expected him to be in bed, but he was nowhere to be found. I looked out to the Jacuzzi; it was empty. But next to it, in the studio, dim light loomed through the window blinds. Sliding the doors off of my bedroom open, I stepped outside and walked to the door. Turning the knob slowly, I peered in. There he was, asleep on a low back, modern, turquoise couch in nothing but a pair of low-slung, black workout pants. As quietly as I could, I stepped back out the door, removed all of my clothing then quietly padded across the wood plank floor.

Standing over him, my heart started beating so loudly, I was surprised it did not wake him. He was so gorgeous and peaceful. I almost didn't want to wake him, but I need him. Lowering myself on to the houndstooth area rug that sat under the couch, I brought my hands to the top of his pants. Untying them, I pulled them down enough to free him. Placing alight kiss on the crown, I felt hands reach me. "Sofie, please tell me I'm not dreaming." His voice was soft and gravely. I looked up to see beautiful lavender eyes.

"I'm real. I'm sorry. I made a mistake. Forgive me."

"Are you done with him?"

"Him?"

"Marco. David told me you left. That Marco picked you up from the airport. That you were safe."

"He did. But, I'm not with him. Marco is your hero. I'm here because of him. You will need to thank him." Drake started to speak, but I extended my finger to his lips. "Let me finish. He made me watch the tape, frame by frame on my sister's huge TV. It was obviously doctored, but the film was really you." This got Drake's full attention. He tried to speak. Again, I shook my head, smiling. "It was you and me. Someone filmed us the night on the set. The girl was added and the first part was added. That wasn't you. Marco and Gracee kept analyzing the first part after they pointed out the birthmark on my hip…"

"Your heart," Drake said softly, reaching his hand to my left hip.

"You noticed it?" I nearly purred feeling his gentle caress.

"I love every inch of you…" he almost whispered. I lowered my head as a couple tears slide down my cheeks. I was so happy, why was I crying? "I love you, Sofie," he said pulling me up so my body covered his. He felt so good, so right.

"I love you, Drake," I whispered against his lips as he cupped my face, before he sunk his teeth into my bottom lip. I moaned and he captured my mouth completely, slipping his pants off. I did my best to assist him. I needed him. I wanted him. He needed to make me his, again.

Chapter Five

DRAKE...

AWAKENING BY MY breathtakingly beautiful Sofie, naked, kneeling on the floor next to me, I thought I had died and gone to heaven. As much as I loved her mouth wrapped around me, I wanted to feel her covering me. Lifting her fit-frame from the rug, she molded to me; the warmth . . . the softness. I held her tight . . . I missed her so much. My heart raced, my cock throbbed with anticipation of taking possession of her completely. Attacking her, I heard our mixed moans and groans; both of us aggressive with our tongues and teeth. It wasn't enough. Once begging escaped Sofie's lips, I grasped her hips firmly while she reached between us, guiding me deep inside. Oh, God, nothing had ever felt so right, so incredible—so mine.

"You're mine." My teeth captured her neck.

"Yes," she panted, "always... always yours."

Her words had me wild. I wanted to stand up, puff out my chest, and thump it with my fists, caveman like . . . Tarzan like . . . King Kong like. I had my Sofie back. I wanted to shout it from the top of the Empire

State Building. Instead, I flipped her onto her back, lifting her feet up on my shoulders. I felt the need to deepen my drive. To take her completely. Fill her. Climb inside of her. I never wanted to be separated again.

WHEN I AWOKE the next morning, I thanked my lucky stars, that the night before was real. She was real; still in my arms, her body half draped over mine, on the sofa, in her studio. Moving, my girl started to slide her body over mine, but I pulled up, causing her to grunt her disapproval. "Where are you going?"

"We. Are. Going to a more comfortable spot." Standing, I reached for her. Despite my aching back from sleeping awkwardly, yet perfectly, I scooped her up. Naked, I walked us across the garden with her tightly to my chest, her arms around my neck, her teeth attacking my left pec. "Sofie, darling, I'm never going to make it to the bed if you keep that up."

She laughed and purred, "Who said we need a bed... the lawn looks fine to me." I shook my head. Ignoring her, I managed to make it up onto the teak deck and through the glass doors to her bedroom. Settling her on the bed, I went in search of sweats to slip on. "Where are you going now?"

"I'm going to get nourishment for our bodies. Stay there. We will be spending the whole day in bed. There is a lot of time to make up," I said with a wink before ducking out of the room. I heard her call after me to hurry back or she would come looking for me.

In the kitchen, I filled the tea kettle with water, turned the burner on, and scooped ground coffee into a copper French press. Next up was the food. I pulled out pre-packages of sliced tropical fruit from the refrigerator. Then I grabbed two berry scones from a glass cake plate that was always displaying sweet treats from a nearby organic bakery. Locating a teakwood tray in the pantry, I placed it on the counter, ready to be filled for breakfast in bed.

Back in the bedroom, I found Sofie under the covers with her eyes closed. Fair enough, we hadn't gotten much sleep on the studio couch. As I was about to back out of the room, her eyes opened, "I'm awake. Was just resting my eyes. Don't leave."

Setting the tray in the middle of the bed, she sat up, allowing the sheet to pool at her waist. I swooped in, giving each of her pretty, pink nipples a little attention before handing her a cup of coffee. Then, I grabbed my own mug, moving to the end of the bed. Leaning against the bed post diagonally across from her, I watched her. She cocked her head sideways. "Why are you so far from me?" she asked, nibbling on a piece of ripe mango. I was tempted to lick the juice that ran down her chin. My reason for distance.

"I want you to eat. Seeing as though it is difficult to keep my hands to myself…"

"Who said they wanted you to keep your hands to

yourself?" She smiled. My heart pounded.

"We have all day. I promise to not leave you alone."

"I missed you."

"I missed you too, Sofie."

Reaching forward, I grabbed one of the scones; she watched my every move. "I see you visited my favorite pastry shop."

"I've kept the house stocked with all of your favorites: flowers, food. I've been ready for your return. I was never ready for your departure."

"I'm sorry…"

"Don't be. I knew there needed to be proof. I've been wracking my brain. Searching for answers. I'd figured it was Blaine. But how? How could I not remember?"

"Hard to remember something that never happened."

"That's true. Yet, it looked so real. I figured I had to be drugged. I mentioned something to the women in the video. They looked at me like I was crazy. Shit! Did Blaine slip something to all of us, I wondered. Getting answers was going to be harder than I imagined. And Lila said…"

"Lila?"

"Don't be mad. I needed another pair of ears and eyes on the set. Someone that I knew was not out to get me. More important—someone on your side. I told her all about the tape. How I lost my phone, or someone stole it, and that you received messages from me . . . but not really me. That I would never willingly hurt you. I asked her to help me without betraying you."

"I'm sorry I shut you out."

"It was understandable. If the tables were turned, I'm not sure how I would've reacted. I'm just happy it's over. When this film wraps, Blaine will have to answer to me . . . to us."

"Blaine-the-pain," she said through gritted her teeth. "What's the story between you two? I've never asked. I was waiting, but…"

"Back when I was working on Dave's student films, Blaine and I became friends. We all seemed to be doing several roles in those days. Whatever we could, to make the film come together. Blaine was working as the cinematographer and film editor. He was the kind of guy that was always looking to get ahead, and looking for a good time. Surfing. Partying. Fucking. Not in any certain order. When I first met him, I was dating this girl whose family was a big deal in the film world. That did not impress me. Nor did she, for very long, when I found out she was more interested in getting Dave jealous…"

"Sounds like Mandolina."

"Exactly!"

"I had no idea you dated her. Ugh! That girl caused so much shit!"

"Yes, so I've heard. Believe me, it was brief. Anyway, as soon as I moved on, Blaine moved in. He wasn't about to miss an opportunity with her father. Mandi, of course, thought it might get Dave's attention. She was wrong, again. Blaine knew what she was up to, but he was going to use her."

"Good! I hope he broke her heart, if she ever had one—what a perfect pair." I watched her take a firm bite of pineapple like she was biting her head off. I had to laugh. I was certain steam would be coming out of her ears, at any moment.

"Are you going to let me finish my story?"

"Sorry . . . go on." She waved her hands in the air. "Tell me."

"So, one night, I'm sitting at home and Blaine shows up. He was definitely on something. All hyped up, he insisted I go to a party with him. He had told me about connections with this person and that person. That night, he wanted me to meet some. What the hell? I had nothing planned. We hopped in his Ferrari and shot over to the Valley. Once we got to the house, I was shocked. There were naked chicks all over the place. In some rooms, right out in the open, people were partaking in different sexual acts…"

"A porn house? Oh. My. God."

"Yes. Blaine was involved in the porn industry before he started taking film classes at UCLA."

"Holy shit!"

"The shit did hit the fan after that night. He confided in me how and when he got involved. He swore me to secrecy. Then somehow, Mandi got word of Blaine's past and she dumped him abruptly. He was devastated. Not because he was attached to her, but he was attached to her father. He, of course, thought that I told her. He accused me of being jealous that her father had taken to him. I was anything but jealous. I didn't need his influence or his help. The film industry was not for me. I did it to help Dave. He ended making a big scene, said I ruined his life, punched me in the face, and then he disappeared. I hadn't seen or heard from him until the night that Dave introduced him as the cinematog at the party."

"I knew he was after you. I never thought he was ever interested in me. He was always so professional . . . a gentleman when you were out of the picture. Once you were anywhere near, he snapped. That wasn't enough to break us apart . . . so . . . so he doctored sex tapes…"

"Lila doesn't believe it's his doing. I wonder if she's a little bias. I think something may be brewing with them."

"Really? I haven't noticed. I actually haven't seen her much. She's usually off doing things for me . . . and apparently, you!"

"And watching him."

"You have Lila spying on him?"

"Yes, I guess I should text her. The jig is up! Let her get back to more important things."

"Maybe not. Might be best to see if he has more tricks up his sleeves. He has been sending you photos of me. Obviously, he's not done."

"That reminds me. We need to find that hidden

camera in your trailer. I don't want films of us popping up. If they aren't, already. And . . . now that we are back together, I want to be able to take full use of your caravan while we're on set. Those were some of the best downtimes I have ever experienced."

"Why don't you remind me," she said, licking her lips. I scurried to her, moving the tray to the floors. Then I reminded her all day and night, breaking only long enough to refuel our bodies with a bevy of food and drink. We celebrated our togetherness privately, anticipating what would happen when we went public. What would be the next blow to our relationship?

BACK ON THE set, we found the mini camera directed at the bed and deposed of it. It appeared that Blaine had given up. We wrapped up filming, moved into post-production and editing. We were often together, the three of us, and others. No incidents. No texts. I was relieved, though part of me still wanted to confront Blaine. I was just waiting for the right moment.

I didn't have to wait too long. A few weeks prior to the premiere of the film, we got together, up at the producer's house, the same place where Blaine was introduced to the cast and crew. One too many drinks, his mouth spewed shit, as always. He really should never drink. Anyway, he made one too many comments to Sofie, pawed her one too many times. I couldn't let it go.

"Blaine, cut the shit. We both know you're not into Sofie, so lay off."

He laughed. "You're right. I don't give a fuck about her—or you. You, Mr. Perfect, never can do no wrong . . . tattletale . . . snoop . . . tell-all. Ha! You think I care? Not I, not me! No, you . . . you and Sofie shouldn't fuck everywhere. I told you. Yes, I knew. I knew you would fuck with the wrong person, one day. You would get was coming to you. You would get caught. Caught right in the act with your pants down." His laughter escalated. "Too bad it wasn't me. No. It's not me."

"Are you sure about that? You didn't want to get even with me? For exposing your secret life? Which I didn't do."

"Nah! You didn't expose me. I thought it was you at first. I was pissed. I lashed out at you. Really, it could've been a number of people. But it happened so close to when I confessed to you, trusted you."

"I hoped you were over it. Then this tape shit."

"Yea. Fuck. I thought I was over it too. Then I saw you at the party. Everyone fawning over you; the women like always, David boosting about you. Listening to the gossip, the buzz that you might be gracing the screen with your acting, again. Then there was the way Sofie looked at you, like you were God. Yes, I was jealous of you. Jealous of you and Sofie. Yes, I was even more jealous of you and David. Yes, I'm an asshole, I know. I just need the right one. I want what you two have. So I'll admit, I messed with you a bit, but the filming? The sex thing? The texts? Not me. Excuse me, I take part back, that was me fucking the two chicks, but I didn't know about the doctoring, the editing, or that I was being filmed. I thought the chicks were part of the scam. They denied everything when I showed them the tape that was also texted to me with a warning to keep my mouth shut. The girls were enraged. They tried to say I drugged them. They claimed they didn't remember. I say they lied. I say they got a big check or a big promise from someone. I can truly say I was pretty fucked up that night…"

"So if it wasn't you, who was it?"

"I would say, someone we all pissed off."

Chapter Six

SOFIE...

ONCE WE FOUND out Blaine was not behind our unwarranted separation, I started receiving some disturbing texts, and Drake became extremely worried for my safety. If he wasn't by my side, a big, burly bodyguard was. It started the night he was leaving to go up North for one last major adjustment that had to be made to the film. His flight had been delayed, due to excessive fog, so one of the producers made arrangements to use his plane. Having extra time, he came back home to wait it out. Taking advantage of those added minutes, he spent it being intimate with me. Entwined was the way we liked to spend our hours, without interruptions. However, it was at a very inopportune moment that texts began, one after another. It was difficult to ignore them.

"Oh, he really did fool you."

"Maybe that was a film with you."

"He won't be yours forever."

"He will see you for who you are; once a tramp, always a tramp."

"Does he know about all of your whoring around?"

"Love them and leave them."

"Maybe there are tapes of you."

"Beware!"

Those messages earned me a trip up North. Not that I minded, I was pretty freaked out, too. Until Drake, I had never had any problems like this. Whoever was behind this had to know both of us. First, they went after him. Then, it appeared, it was my turn. What would make them give up? If we were to split up completely, would they be satisfied? I was scared. I prayed that this wouldn't turn violent. Hopefully, it was just a scorned lover that would give up. Not some crazy psychopath. Whoever it was that continued to send texts to me and then to Drake, hadn't truly thought their actions through. Instead of tearing us apart, it was bringing us closer.

Two days before the film's premiere, we had to alert David. We had both received similar texts that sounded like the person behind everything would be attending the evening's events. I had never seen David so mad, ever. He laid into both of us for keeping him in the dark all of this time. After he calmed down, he secured extra security for the theatre, red carpet, and the after party. Along with uniformed attendants, he called in some favors, and had all of the locations searched ahead of time. Fortunately, nothing turned up. One problem down. Next, we waited to see if anyone would step forward, or would they remain in the shadows, taunting us?

The morning of the event, pampering was the name of the game; Drake and I had massages, followed by lunch. Then I went off to Nelle's salon to get the works: Manicure, pedicure, hair, and makeup. Back home, I carefully slid into a tub to refresh my body. Out of my bath, I dried, lotioned, and slipped into a black, fitted, just above the knee, cocktail dress. Then I adorned my feet with a pair of black Bionda Castana Beatrix heels. Ready to go, I found an extremely handsome man waiting for me in a tailored black suit with a silver tie and matching pocket square. He looked good enough to stay home. To hell with the premiere, I thought. But then again, I was overly excited to experience my first red carpet in a major role. Granted, no one would recognize me as I promenaded by them, but I knew my name would be up on the silver screen. I couldn't wait to see the film with an audience. I couldn't keep from smiling.

"You look stunning, Sofie." Standing, he made his way to me. A light kiss to my lips sent chills down my spine.

"You are quite dapper, this evening." I grasped the arm he had extended to me, and we strolled to a waiting car.

The red carpet made me nervous and giddy all at once. There was action all around. Television Crews. Photographers. Interviewers. Celebrities. Gowns. Fans screaming. Total excitement as we glided toward the entrance of Grauman's Chinese Theatre. A venue that David and the executive producers had selected, only a short few steps away from the Dolby Theatre, yes, home of the Academy Awards.

Watching the film with a live audience was amazing. I'm not sure if I paid full attention to the screen. I was listening for the laughter, the screams, the cries, the oohs, and the aahs. Any and all emotion. I wanted to know that they were feeling things in all of the right places, by hearing their responses. When the picture ended and the credits rolled, I smiled seeing, "Production Designer Sofie James." I saw it at the beginning on the film, but seeing it again made it more real! As we filed out to the lobby, I eased dropped on conversations. Comments abound. Most of them were a delight to hear. Some, not as great, but still, they had an opinion. I was beaming; walking on cloud nine.

Leaving the Chinese theatre, we hopped in to our waiting car that took us a couple blocks away to a historical concert hall for the celebration to begin. Another, smaller red carpet, directed us to a reception area, set up outside of an established dining room, where champagne and appetizers were presented by tuxedoed men. We enjoyed milling around, chatting with fellow cast and crew, along with critics. I loved the buzz of the room, it was filled with energy. People were happy. It was a party. What could go wrong?

Once the drapery opened, everyone found their assigned seat for dinner. Seated, I took in the all of the spectacular decor. It was exquisite. Midnight-blue velvet drapery walled the space. Huge Italian crystal chandeliers hung at different lengths around the room, lighting the silvery-blue dressed tables with gold bamboo chairs. Bold purple and apple green floral arrangements added dramatic color to the overall design. I nudged Drake when the food was served, Steak Oscar—filet mignon topped with crab meat and asparagus. That had to be David's selection. I hoped he was channeling the Oscar Gods in his favor. Whomever he had hired for this event had done a stupendous job, so far, and it continued with the entertainment. A laser light show and DJ had everyone up out of their seats and moved on to a lounge area, complete with sofas surrounding a dance floor, and stage. Drake and I took to the dance floor off and on. I loved the few slow songs, any excuse to rub up against my yummy man. The night was completely perfect . . . or at least part of it was.

Walking off the dance floor, we were greeted. Well, greeted might not have been the right word. "Oh, if it isn't the happy fucking couple. Doesn't anything bad ever happen to you, Drake? Always the perfect life." The voice was gravelly with a hint of slur mixed in for good . . . bad measure.

"Always a pleasure to see you, too. Is life treating you well?" Drake flashed a hard-pressed smile in her direction.

"Cut the small talk; acting like you give a fuck about me. Your movie has been funded—made—no need to suck up to me. Oh. Speaking of movies, I heard about a little sex tape scandal. Too bad it wasn't true, or too bad you figured out the truth." The drunk woman teetered on her high Manolo pumps in a short, low-cut, dark-red, lace dress with a glass swirling in her hand.

"Nice to hear your concern, Mandolina," I said, knowing she hated her given name.

Turning toward me, her eyes narrowed. "Mandi."

"Oh, yes, of course. Silly me." I stifled a laugh as she let out a hmphf sound.

"You and Drake, you two fucked things up for me and David." My back straightened as her volume increased. Where was all of this coming from? She hadn't been with him in more than ten years. As I was assembling words to ask, her she turned back to Drake. "He could've been jealous of you, but you wouldn't play along."

Drake didn't miss a beat when he calmly replied adamantly, "Maybe if he was interested in you, but he never was."

Ignoring Drake's words, Mandi tipped back her glass, placed it on a passing tray, and grabbed for a new one. Thinking this gave us time to escape, I tried to move away, but Drake didn't budge. "Blaine was a fucking waste of time. I used him best I could. No relying on any of you." She was wicked. Her laughter with an evil undertone, gave me goose-bumps. "I lured David to my house once, telling him Daddy wanted to talk to him. He came running. Everyone ran when my father's name was mentioned. Of course, he was not home. He rarely was. Anyway, I offered David a drink while he waited for Daddy, who wasn't going to appear. It was easy to drug him. He lost his clothes . . . all his inhibitions. I prayed that this would do it. Let me be pregnant. But no..."

"Oh my God," escaped my lips before I could stifle my thoughts.

"Yes. Imagine. Your little matchmaking between David and his precious Nelle wouldn't have worked so well if I was carrying his bastard." A purely sinister look was painted on her face. I wondered how much alcohol she had consumed or was she nasty naturally?

I didn't know Mandi very well, nor did I want to, after this run-in. I had been forced to socialize with her on a few rare occasions. Mainly, I had only heard of her stunts, first from David and then, from Nelle. David had complained about her at one time, when he was first dating his wife. She had worked her way into Nelle's graces, feeding her lies about her relationship with David. When that didn't work, she followed them around. Got herself on the guest list of events they attended. When David announced their engagement after only dating for a short period, she finally backed off.

However, as she continued to drone on about him, it was apparent, she had never truly gotten over him. "Yes, I followed him. I heard him speaking about a party. I sat outside his apartment one night, waiting for his car to leave the building. I followed him to the Valley. Then down a long driveway. I parked, waited, then walked in to quite a scene. It was not one I would ever imagine Mr. Goody-Two-Shoes attending. I was right. Turns out, he traded cars with Blaine to impress the little bitch with a Ferrari. Ha! He could've had his own, if he picked me. Oh well, dumbshit..." Taking a big swig of bubbly, she then continued, "Speaking of dumbshits . . . Blaine . . . good ol' Blaine. He really is of no use, is he? He does have friends in the right places, though. Thanks to him, I met Rowan. Oh, don't look puzzled, Rowan shoots porn films. He's brilliant. Perfect for splicing together your scene. If only I had Rowan make a sex tape of David and me. That could've come in handy. Maybe then, he and Danelle would never have gotten together." She laughed so hard, it caused her a stagger a bit. Gentleman that Drake is, he reached out and steadied her on her feet. I would rather she fell, so we could've walk away.

"When I found out my father was investing in David's film project, I felt some old familiar tingles, but they quickly fizzled out. Of course, Mr. and Mrs. Maxsam were still happily married with a new baby on the way, I see. But, then I heard you..." she said, nearly poking me in the chest, taking another gulp. "You and Drake were onboard. Then, next, came Blaine—well, fuck me—all the people that fucked me over. It was time to call up a certain someone and blackmail another. God, Blaine was so easy to manipulate . . . and starlets . . . dumb cunts . . . they will fuck anything and everybody to get ahead. And then, there is you! You and Drake really should be careful, fucking in public . . . people have cameras in their phones . . . security cameras are just about everywhere . . . sets . . . trailers. . ." She laughed smugly, slurring one thought into another.

"So Blaine was not behind all of this crap?" I asked, wanting to pull her hair, and slap that happy look right off of her face.

"Ha! He was useful, but other than that, no. I knew he wouldn't resist two women, wanting to fuck him on film. Besides, I told him Drake spread rumors about him years ago. I told him that he also warned me to stay away from Blaine or he would tell my father that I was dating a porn maker. He was more than happy to ruin your romance like he thought you broke ours up. Not that we were in love. Far from it."

"Text messages? Drake's phone?" She wanted to tell all; I wanted to know everything.

"One of the whorelettes lifted it for me. Funny, Blaine's vocabulary was so predictable . . . so easy to duplicate."

"Why come clean now?" Drake inquired.

"Not my idea. Daddy told me if I wanted to continue to receive his assistance... money," she laughed, draining her glass. "And for some ungodly reason, my father is enchanted with Blaine and his camera work. I got fucked again and dumbshit Blaine is getting the deals of a lifetime, apparently, so are both of you. I can't fucking win . . . so there you have it . . . my confession. Maybe I better make sure Daddy hears it. Where is my wonderful father?"

Pushing off of Drake, she attempted to set down her latest empty glass. Unsuccessful; it crashed to the ground, causing those close by to take notice. Weaving her way toward the elaborate DJ stage, she grabbed a champagne bottle off of a low cocktail table and continued on. Teetering on her high heels, she began to climb up the steps to the stage. Oh shit, what was she going to do now? She stopped briefly, looking around. Then, began up another set of stairs that lead to several different, level, platforms surrounding the DJ and housing equipment that provided the light show, accompanying the music. Stopping on the next level, she appeared to be yelling. With the music playing, her voice was drown out. Drake tried yelling up to her, "Mandi, get down." It was of no use, she couldn't hear him. I could barely hear him, standing so close to a multitude of booming speakers.

It wasn't long before she was kicking off her shoes, hitting the DJ as they went flying. "Oh shit! How the hell? What the hell is she doing up there?" loomed from the DJ's mouth. Stopping his music, he shouted into his microphone. "Fuck! Someone needs to get her! She shouldn't be up there. It's too dangerous. Lots of cords. Wires..." Time seemed to have stood still, people had turned to look up, their eyes glued to the crazy woman, high above, swinging a champagne bottle. Silence fell over the crowd. "Please get down," the DJ requested.

"It's okay . . . I'm fine. Just looking for my daddy..." Mandi replied, then looked out to the audience, she was holding captive. "Where are you, Daddy?" It appeared she wasn't satisfied with her view as she tossed the champagne bottle and began scaling the scaffolding high above the stage area. The DJ began yelling for help.

Finally, her father had stalked across the dance floor. "Mandolina Alexandria, climb down from there, at once."

His words stopped her climbing. Holding on to a pole with one hand, she held her other one up to her brow, gazing down to her father below. "Oh, Daddy, look at your pretty, little princess… I confessed… No more problems… Just a good girl, Daddy…" Mandi was laughing and slurring, hanging on to scaffolding, precariously.

Her father moved over closer to us. He was looking for a way up. "How did she get up there?" He asked one of the DJ's grips who had walked from behind the stage to see what was going on. "You need to get someone up there to help her, now!" His voice was strong, full of agitation. He was waving his arms, breathing hard.

Drake started to move, looking around. "No, don't you dare." I didn't want Drake trying to be a hero. Nor did I want him to get hurt, attempting to help that crazy woman.

"Don't worry; I'm not going up there. Let me find some security guys."

"Please don't leave me." I held onto his bicep tightly, then, pointed at a team of uniformed men, heading toward the stage on both sides, "Here comes some help."

However, before anyone could get to her we all watched as she wobbled about, stumbling, trying to adjust her footing onto another ladder. Then with a slip of her hand, a blood curdling scream escaped from her mouth as she started to plummet to the ground. Drake quickly turned me into his chest, blocking my view. The sound was sickening. I clung to him, crying.

Security scrambled to her lifeless body. Her father was hot on their heels, shouting for someone to call 911. By the time the paramedics had arrived, Mandi was not breathing and she had no pulse. Security had done their best with administering CPR. But it was no use; the paramedics calmly indicated that she had broken her neck in the fall. Her father did not listen. He insisted that they work on her. Appeasing him, they secured her with a neck brace, strapped onto a back board, and wheeled her to a waiting ambulance. But it was too late. The damage had been done. The evening was over for all of us. The celebration had turned to a time of mourning. All I wanted to do was escape, to be alone with Drake.

Making our way out of the party, we headed for home. Once we arrived, Drake guided me to my bedroom. Undressing, we climbed into bed and held each other, not saying a word. I was shocked. I was sad. I didn't know what to say . . . what to think. But I knew Mandi did not deserve to die for her actions. As much as I despised what she had done to so many people over the years, I never wished her harm. I may have hoped that she got what was coming to her, but definitely nothing . . . nothing like that. Wrapped up in the safety of Drakes' strong arms, clinging to him, I closed my eyes, and sobbed, until sleep overtook me.

Chapter Seven

DRAKE...

THE DAY AFTER the premiere, the entertainment page headlines read, Hit in the Midst of Tragedy. The article went on to tell the tale of the evening's events with a bit of a twist. It was reported that the daughter of a certain, well-known, film producer had fallen to her death while dancing, high above, on a platform stage at the movie premiere after-party. The story continued with rave reviews of the film, followed by a write-up, outlining the life of a lovely, young woman and her untimely death. Nothing was mentioned about her recklessness. Her intoxication. Her nasty disposition. She was painted as a perfect daughter—her father's little princess. Which, was all well and good for her parents. Whom, I'm sure, did not want the gory truth spilled about their daughter, and perhaps paid to keep it that way—for as long as they could. There were always people that were perpetually looking for dirt; scandal.

One of the sickest parts about this whole unfortunate incident was that some people involved in the production said that maybe we should thank her for drawing attention to the film. "Death equals Oscar," someone whispered. All of this, and more, I overheard, believe it or not, at her memorial service. While I wasn't fond of Mandi, I knew her parents were grieving, and I hoped that these remarks were not hitting their ears. As mad as I was at what she had done, hurting so many people over the years, I didn't wish death upon her. I would've preferred that she received the help she so obviously needed.

After Mandi's funereal, I was even more certain I had made the right decision about accepting an outstanding project in Boston that had been offered to me. This Hollywood crowd was still rubbing me the wrong way, after all these years. Don't get me wrong, I loved the making of films as much as I did in the beginning, but besides the creativity, I could easily walk away, again. There was only one major problem—Sofie.

Since the opening-night premiere, the worldwide release, the Oscar-potential buzz, and the infamous publicity that surrounded the film, several movie deals along with scripts had been messengered. Sofie was finally given the recognition she so craved. The type of jobs she desired, were being placed in her hands. She had choices. I even received a few film offers; some for acting and some for set designing. I was quick to decline all of them.

During the time that Sofie and I were apart, I was offered some big architectural projects. One of which, I could not turn down. Being away from her, gave me time to start working on it. Like Sofie's desire to be a production designer, the job handed to me was my dream project. I had bid on it years ago. However, the City of Boston had stopped plans and refused to budge until the building, in question, was starting to come apart at the seams. The thought of losing a historical landmark had the City contacting my architectural firm. One of my partners contacted me with the incredible news. He knew all about the drawings I had worked on, along with all of the time and energy I had put into research for rejuvenating and enhancing the building. I could not say no. I had to leave. I needed to get back to my firm . . . to the job of my lifetime. It was easy to say yes a couple months ago when I thought I had lost Sofie forever. Once she returned to me, the reality set, hit me . . . there was a deadline for my return to Boston.

FOR OUR REMAINING time together, unbeknownst to her, I was always looking for the right time. I was constantly on the brink of pounding my head against the wall. There just wasn't a perfect moment. There was no prefect solution. I don't know what I could've been thinking about, when I decided to come to LA. To be honest, at first, I was thinking with my cock. Then, my heart. But I, definitely, never used my head. I hadn't really thought pass the project. Spending a year with Sofie, working with her day in, day out. Going to bed with her in my arms. Waking up curved around her luscious body. The reality of leaving her was devastating. I couldn't imagine giving her up. We had to work this out, somehow. But, could we work it out? A bi-coastal relationship; flying out to each other whenever we could? Funny, it seemed as if I had had this conversation with myself, not that long ago. I wasn't looking forward to having it with Sofie.

What was the best way to break the news to her? This question haunted me, daily. A romantic getaway was the answer I came up with. I thought, maybe breaking the news to her would be easier if we were neutral ground. Would that really matter? I asked myself, as we drove up the Coast and over again, the next day, while we were hiking. When would be the right time? Would it ruin one of our last weekends together? Do I announce it over dinner? Driving up? Driving home? Ha! In bed . . . no, definitely not in bed.

"Are you okay, Drake? You're so quiet." Sofie ran her fingertip over my forearm as we looked out over a stream, running in the valley below.

I wanted to turn. I wanted to look at her, but I was afraid to gaze into those green eyes of hers, when I broke the news. "I told you about the theatre, the one in my office…" No time like the present, I had to spill all now. "My drawings are finally going to become a reality."

As I paused to search my next words, she questioned, "What? I thought you designed that?"

Shaking my head, I grasped her hand, pulling her to

a big rock. Leaning against it, I spread my legs. I loved how she moved right in between. Wrapping my arms around, I took in a deep breath. "I didn't think you were listening to me that day in my office. Now, I know I was right."

As Sofie let out a light laugh, I bent toward her, capturing her lip between my teeth. Lightly tugging, I felt her tongue skim my mouth. I was ready to devour her right then and there, but she leaned back, and I was suddenly sorry that I had started this conversation.

"Alright. I will confess. I wasn't listening to you. I find it hard to concentrate at times while I'm looking at you..." Her fingers were playing with my hair. I wanted to rewind. Fast forward. "I did make a mental note to search the internet for the building..." God, she smelled... oh, so good. It was my turn—I was the one not paying attention. "I'm sorry. I have another confession. I forgot."

"You forgot what?"

"You're not listening to me, now." She smiled, slapping my chest. I pulled her closer, hugging her tightly, up against my body. "I said I forgot to research the theatre."

"You would've never found it." I rested my chin on top of her head as I continued. "Well, that's not entirely true. You may have found the original building, but not the renderings on my wall. Those were solely my vision."

Softly she commented, "They're beautiful."

"Thank you. They are what I imagined when I came

across an abandoned, Boston theatre, when I first started working at the firm. I visited it on several more occasions. Photographed it at every angle. Back in the office, I began to sketch ideas. I did research. Got blueprints. I even gained access to the inside with my father's help. It was a mess. It is a mess. Worse than the first time I saw it." I stopped to place a kiss on the top of her head. The hard part was drawing near. A lump in my throat. "It became my obsession when I wasn't working on regular jobs. Once I was satisfied, I showed everything to Patrick. He was impressed. I think it was my gateway; the deciding factor to me becoming a partner in the firm. Anyway, he secured a meeting with City officials. We presented the plans. We were denied for years, until…"

"Until?" She tried to look up at me. I kept her tucked into me.

"About six weeks ago . . . maybe seven. The City of Boston gave us the green light. They were finally allowing the building to be updated. Renovated. Actually they had no choice, when a portion fell. The possibility of a lawsuit, not to mention, the loss of the historical site, was not something they wanted to deal with. Luckily, they were also willing to waive some of their strict policies about the exterior renovations. This would give way to some of my designs. Of course, we would keep the same integrity… My firm partners knew, based on my extensive drawings, I was the one to head the project. My love of the building…" Deep breath. "I . . . I couldn't turn it down… I can't walk away…"

"Was that why I found you in the studio? With drawings spread all around?" She pulled back. This time I knew I had to let her, even though; I didn't want to see the look in her face. I nodded.

"You're already deep in…" Her voice was shaky.

"Sofie," I moved my hands up to hold her face in my hands. "I love you. I don't want to leave you, but Hollywood's not for me. I'm going home."

She reached up and held my wrists. "I understand . . . I do."

"This is the hardest thing I have ever had to do in my life. I'm not leaving you. I would never leave you." I rested my forehead on hers. The look in her eyes was killing me. "In the same breath, I would never ask you to walk away from your life . . . your career, here. I've been trying to figure out a way for us to make this work. I've been in LA for a year."

She nodded. "I know."

"God, Sofie, it has been the best and the worst time of my life. I miss my life in Boston. I can't lie. I have a company I need to get back to. My time is up. As much as I don't want to leave you, I have to."

I thought I would die on the spot, when she leaned back. Looking at me with glassy eyes, her bottom lip tucked under her top one, she nodded her head. Then stroking my cheek with her hand, she reassured me. She comforted me. "I understand. I really do."

"We will make this work. I promise. We are not saying goodbye." I pulled back into my arms. I never wanted to let go.

"I'll come visit. You can give me more lessons in architecture," she laughed softly.

"Fair warning, if you ever come to Boston, I don't think I will ever let you go. I love you so much, Sofie."

"Don't tell me, show me."

"Right here? Right now?" I asked, grinning.

Lifting her head, she spoke, staring up at me. "Yes. Out in the open." Reaching up, she wrapped her fingers around my neck, pulling my face to hers. "Show me . . . show everyone how much you love me."

Excepting her invitation, I attacked her mouth and she counterattacked. Our kiss was frantic with teeth, tongues, and moans. I couldn't get her undressed quick enough. We could've been discreet, but I needed to feel all of her. Her skin on mine. Her breasts against my chest. My cock against her mound. Lifting her up, she wrapped her legs around my waist and I plunged in. Rocking into her, feeling her body tighten around me, I didn't give a fuck who was around as I united our bodies. They could arrest me for indecent exposure—lewd acts in public, but they would have to wait until I finished. I was willing to be charged further with resisting arrest. It would be worth it. Every fine I would have to pay. Every courtroom I would have to visit. I did my best to show Sofie just how much I loved every inch of her.

Luck was on our side, not another soul was spotted in the vicinity as we came down from our high. Dressed once again, we made our way back to the car, and eventually to our hotel room where we remained for the rest of the weekend. Fueled by room service, I continued to express my love for Sofie over and over again to the point of, blissful, exhaustion. Exploring every nook and cranny of her body, claiming every part of her—she was completely mine. By Sunday afternoon, we practically crawled out of our room, to make our way home. Driving, I wished that we had arranged transportation with a driver.

For the next few weeks, Sofie and I spent every moment together. She poured over scripts in the studio while I worked on my project. I loved her interest in every aspect of my upcoming job. I secretly wished that she would work with me on it. Yet, I could not say those words. I could not pressure her. Make her feel guilty. I just enjoyed our time together.

The morning of my departure, I told her I couldn't bear saying goodbye at the airport, a car had been hired. She begged me to cancel. Promised she wouldn't make a scene. "No crying, I promise," she said. However, I couldn't promise that. I had been choking back tears since I told her I was leaving. Giving in to my decision, she walked me outside, holding my hand tightly. Stopping in front of the opened car door, I took her in my arms, crushing my mouth to hers. Such sweet lips, I would miss. Reluctantly, I let her go. Then, with tears in both of our eyes, I turned and climbed into my waiting town-car.

Chapter Eight

SOFIE...

SITTING AT MY lonely, kitchen nook table, looking at a stack of scripts, things felt so wrong. His seat was empty. I was empty. I couldn't believe it. Everything I ever wanted was right at my fingertips. Finally, I was receiving jobs offers I had only ever dreamt about. I was being commended on my work. I should've been overjoyed. Yet, I craved, I desired . . . I loved living with Drake more. I missed him, I ached for him . . . I longed for my lavender-eyed man. Sighing heavily, I took a sip of my iced coffee. Iced coffee. It was Fall, I should've been drinking hot chocolate, hot tea . . . hot coffee, but it was nearly one hundred degrees. Typical LA weather. What I was used to, not what I wanted.

Looking out my window, I observed lush greenery, and I wondered what color the trees were in The Commons. Were they changing already? Were the leaves decorating the park; littering the grass, the pavement . . . the pond? Were children collecting them? Were they building piles of them? Were they jumping in them? Listening to the sound of their crunchy noise? I closed my eyes. I envisioned the smiles on their tiny faces. Such delight. I could hear the laughter. I smiled to myself. Then I felt the tears that flowed from my eyes cascading down my cheeks.

The thoughts, the daydreams—they weren't enough. No, I needed to experience them, first hand. I needed to be with Drake. He said we would work it out. He loved me. I loved him. We would see each other, when we could. We would savor every moment we could. I didn't want moments. I wanted every day. Yet, here I sat, all alone. Looking around my house, I hated it—everything about it. It was cold. It was not me. It was a stop. It was temporary. Not like us. I wanted warmth. I wanted us. I wanted always . . . forever.

What was I doing? We had to make this work. I had to make this work. I couldn't ask him to stay—to give up his dream. He had sacrificed for me. He had compromised his company for me. He had pulled strings. Now, it was my turn. I couldn't lose him. I had to do something. Suddenly, it was clear to me; I knew what I needed to do. With my decision made, I picked up the phone, and got busy, making calls.

First, I went behind his back as he did to me. Turnabout was fair play. I contacted Patrick, a partner of his I had met on a few occasions, in the architectural firm. I asked that he keep our conversation private. I explained my situation with Drake. I also told him what he had done for me. Some, of which, he already knew since Drake had asked for a leave of absence a little over a year ago. Making a bold move, I inquired about securing a position on Drake's dream theatre project. Knowing that I had a theatrical design background, Patrick was quick to offer me the position of theatre expert advisor. They had been looking for someone who knew what theatre groups would require to make a fully functional setting: the stage, the acoustic, the backstage needs, lighting, etc., etc.

"Sign me. Send me the contract. I'm yours. But, please allow me to tell Drake. I prefer to remain anonymous until I have everything lined up."

I heard a belly-ache laugh escape Patrick's lips, along with the words, "With great pleasure. Do as you will."

Once I learned more about the steps they were taking, it was easy to see that I could work from my home while I got things in order. They faxed, emailed, and messengered me copies of drawings, sketches, and photos. With my camp set up in my studio, I began to research, study, and make notes. During this time, between designing for Drake, I tied up loose ends. I contacted David about my decision, regarding production design job. I hired Gracee's company to sell my house because, of course, she had taken off for San Francisco again. I really need to find out more about her situation, I thought as I took inventory of what was in my home. I had to decide what I wanted and what I didn't for my bold and exciting new adventure—my new future.

I felt so happy, every morning that I woke up. I was

thrilled to be hired, quietly. I loved that the firm had informed Drake that they went ahead and secured a theatre expert. They let him know that the new hire would be looking over his prior work. They said they thought that he would enjoy working with the expert. At this time, communication would need to be via email until the expert could make arrangements to relocate. I loved the idea of him moaning about them going over his head. It was wonderful, knowing I was right when he complained to me during one of our nightly conversations. I had to bite my lip, trying not to laugh. One night, he pushed me to the edge; I almost confessed.

Drake was telling me all about his events of the day. Then he let words slip from his mouth that would've killed me, had I not already secured my position. Although, in the very same breath, I adored them, too. "I start work soon with the theatre expert. I'm really not looking forward to it. I keep thinking, he won't be you. My greatest wish would've been to hire you for the position." A big sigh could be heard as he continued. "I'm sorry, Sofie. I shouldn't put that guilt on you. I know I could never ask you to give up your career to help me."

I was smiling on the outside, knowing he would be getting his wish, but on the inside I had a tightness in my chest. This conversation was bringing me to tears. I felt terrible, stringing him along. I had to hang up abruptly. It truly pained me to keep the secret from him. Hearing such sadness in his voice. I had to tell myself, "Hang in there, the end result would be worth it."

ONCE MY FIRST problem was solved and the solution was moving along smoothly, I had to move on to my next obstacle or challenge. I would need someone who knew Drake well. His father seemed to be the logical choice. I had met Charles a couple of times in the last year. Once, when we visited him on the Cape and once, when he and his wife, Vivian, had a layover in LA before going on to Hong Kong. We got along quite well. He was very easy to speak to, and he had told me thank you for coming into his son's life. Sounded like he would be willing to help me put my plans into motion. Some of which, I would need inside information.

With a little apprehension, I got the courage to call his father at his auction house. He was very cordial and polite, letting me outline what I had done, along with my overall idea. To my utter delight, and I believe his, he agreed to assist me. I breathed a big sigh of relief when he said yes. A bit of a surprise, however, was when I received the offer of a place to stay. Along with this acceptance came daily phone calls from his wife. She updated me with details about how things were going on their end. As each day passed, I grew more eager to get there, as well as nervous. I think the reassurance from Charles and Vivian helped calm me and the fact that she told me constantly, "We can hardly wait until you arrive. Drake is miserable." The second part of her reminder was making me feel warm and fuzzy. I still felt bad about deceiving him.

The night I touched down at Logan Airport, in Boston, is when things finally seemed real. The weeks before, I functioned in a complete fog. I was focused on making everything right. Some days, I had forgotten to eat. Some nights, I barely slept. My mind was forever reeling, working on overtime. I didn't realize what I was doing to my body until I saw the look on Vivian's face. "Oh, my dear, we need to fatten you up. Those bags under your eyes? Not sure who looks worse, you or Drake."

How did it not hit me? She was right; my clothes were hanging on me. It took someone telling me. I was suddenly exhausted. Overcome by emotions, I burst into tears when her arms encircled me. I hadn't seen Drake in a few weeks. I missed him. I was tired of our little visits. I couldn't do a weekend here and there. Going back and forth was killing me. Since we met, almost a year and a half ago, we had had a series of goodbyes. Too many uncertainties. I wasn't willing to do it anymore. Hence: my big decision. Being there, in the airport, on that very night, it hit me hard and the dam of relief broke.

Over that weekend, I was nurtured and pampered. I slept ten hours the first night, eight the next two nights. When I was awake: breakfast, lunch and dinner were catered to me—everything delicious. Along with food and sleep, a day at a lovely health spa was provided. I was groomed from top to bottom, compliments of Charles and Vivian. By the time Monday morning rolled around, my first day of meetings with Patrick, on the actual job site, I felt like a new person.

Hailing a taxi to the theatre, we drove right in front of Drake's place. Silly me almost ducked as if he would notice me. He had no idea I was in Boston. I spoke to him this morning, as usual. He told me his plans for the day. I told him semi-truths. He was going to be in meetings all day. I said me too. "New project, again?" he asked in a strange voice. I was worried he was catching on. However, his voice hinted at anger? Unhappiness? Not sure, but different.

"Yes. Meeting with some key players, today. Things should get moving soon." I tried to be vague and upbeat.

"Good for you…" I heard him cover the phone, speaking to someone in the office. "Gotta run, Sofie… Have a good day… Hope you get what you want."

I was taken aback by his tone. What had happened? "You have a good day, too. I miss you."

"Okay, bye." Just like that, he hung up. No "I miss you too." He didn't even allow me enough time to me "goodbye." The worst part was no "I love you." Something we had been saying on a regular basis.

I needed to hurry up my final plan. First, I met with Patrick, another partner, and a few of the crew members. They showed me around the theatre: outside, seating areas on all three levels, the stage and backstage. Next, they rolled out the final plans which they designed, taking into consideration, my drawings and suggestions. The project was massive. It would be stunning when all was said and done. Drake's dream theatre was going to be a reality, and I was thrilled to be a part of it. At the end of our meeting, Patrick treated me to a lovely lunch. We laughed and joked that we could add espionage to our resumes. It was funny, at the time, but then it hit me. What was Drake going to think? More so, what was up with him and his attitude? I had one part of my plan down; I need to devise the big one.

Later that evening, I had dinner with Vivian. Charles called to say that he needed to meet with Drake, whom never responded to my texts the rest of the day. I felt like crying. I knew I had not made a mistake; taking the job, coming to Boston, but maybe the way I was coming into his life was not the right approach. I couldn't second guess, at this point. I had to move forward. The question was, how would I surprise him?

On the theatre job site?

As he did to me.

Picnic basket in his office?

Oh, how he loved those lunch deliveries.

Supper, waiting for him in his townhouse?

A repeat candlelight dinner; roasted duck, wine.

Invitation to breakfast at our favorite diner?

Sherry would be thrilled to see us together.

Those were all good ideas. Yet, not the right one… Then it hit me… Yes, that was the only place!

Chapter Nine

DRAKE...

M Y THEATRE PROJECT was moving along smoothly. All green lights. People were on the go. Things were happening. We had our regular slew of team players, along with theatre experts (sound people, lighting people, interior design people, etc.) brought in by our theatre consultant, whom I had yet to meet. He seemed to always be out of reach. We communicated mainly through a multitude of emails. He had great ideas. Over the top. Amazon. Where Patrick found him, I had no idea. I was fine with his work. He listened to everything I said. Had great input to my suggestions, visions. No problems whatsoever. Gave me no shit. Got his crew moving. So if I never met him, no big deal. I just wished it was Sofie. I wished she was in charge. I didn't have the heart to ask her. I only ever hinted.

Speaking of my girl, I hadn't heard from Sofie in several days. She told me she had started a big project that required extra attention. She may be out touch here and there, but she would do her best to text me if she couldn't call. She always made sure to tell me she loved me. I did the same. We were seeing each other, when we could, until the beginning of whatever she had accepted. She was pretty quiet about it. Unusual. We had always shared with each other, I missed it. Before she came back on the grid, she said we'd see each other soon. "I promise," were her last words. I liked those, but I wanted to hear her voice. We had talked almost every day since I left. We were back to phone sex. Working out breaks in our schedules, we saw each other a few times.

Last time I saw her almost a month ago, when she invited me to Florida to meet her family for Thanksgiving. We had a great time, but then we were back to standing in an airport saying goodbye. I told her I hoped she would come to Boston for Christmas but she said she couldn't promise anything. I thought we were getting somewhere when she had me to a family gathering, but our careers continued to keep us apart. She hadn't told me much about her latest commitment, but she said it was a dream job. Her and her damn dream jobs. I wanted to scream.

I'll admit, I was a bit of an asshole when Sofie called me this morning, after not hearing from her all weekend. Which really pissed me off—she rarely worked weekends. What the hell was she up to? Was it just too much to deal with; this bi-coastal relationship bullshit? I knew it was getting to me. I needed some advice. Some reassuring. I called my father. I told him I was hoping we could get together. I needed to talk. I couldn't take it anymore. Maybe he could give me some pointers.

Thankfully, he was available.

"Okay, Dad, I'll swing by, after I get out of my last meeting."

"No!" he exclaimed loudly, startling me.

"Okay…"

"Vivian has girlfriends, staying over, from out of town. Actually, I could use a little guy time. I'll meet you at the pub around the corner from my office."

Finishing up a discussion with a couple gentleman from the City zone department, I shook both of their hands, thanked them, and strolled out of their office on Beacon Street. Needing to clear my head, I walked to the pub, passing the Frog Pond, filled with ice skaters of all shapes and sizes. I wished Sofie could see them. See our pond, frozen. I needed to apologize to her, but first, I needed to talk to my father.

Sitting at the bar, we ate dinner, drank a few beers, and I opened up to my father. I told him how I talked to Sofie on the phone and then ignored her all day. So unlike me, my father said. He was right. I even went as far as to say, maybe I just couldn't be with a career woman. Then, I asked how the hell he and my mother did it? Oh, yes, he reminded me—they fought. Bottom line, he asked me if I loved her. Could I live without her? Could I imagine her with another man?

After I answered all of his questions, he simply stated, "Call her. Tell her you love her. Go from there." That's exactly what I did when I got home, only to receive no response.

THE NEXT DAY, I got up and still no text. Shit! I really had fucked up. Dragging myself into work, I hoped for distractions. It proved to be a quiet day. By late afternoon, I was ready to get out of there. Then, the thought of returning to an empty house struck me. Picking up a frame off of my desk, I stared at a photo of Sofie, and contemplated working late. On what, I had no clue.

My shitty mood was interrupted by a knocking on my door, followed by my secretary opening it. Behind her was a delivery man, carrying a large package. "It's heavy, where do you want it?" Instructing him to place it on the coffee table off to the side, he announced it was an urgent matter, pointing to the "open immediately" marked all over the box. Hmm... I wasn't expecting anything. Nor did I want anything. The box I would want delivered to my office would be much larger, and contain Sofie.

After signing for the delivery, he reminded me to open it now, then, left the same way he came in. Walking over to the box with a pair of scissors, I cut through the clear packing tape. Opening the box, inside was another white box. Lifting it out of the brown cardboard shipping box, I kicked the outside package on the floor and set the box back on the table. Flipping off the lid, a folded brown, blue, and lavender tartan patterned wool scarf sat on top. Removing it from the box, I found a brand new pair of black hockey skates, like the ones of my youth. Beneath them was a printed invitation.

Bundle Up!
You are cordially invited
Tuesday, December 16th
6 o'clock in the evening
The Boston Common Frog Pond

With a smile on my face, I tied the skates together, pulled on my overcoat, and wrapped the scarf around my neck. Walking out of my office, I bid my secretary a good night, heading out of the office. I needed to make a stop before proceeding on to the pond. It had to be Sofie, I thought as I made my way home, quickly. Walking in through the front door of my townhouse, I swear I could smell Sofie. It had to be my brain . . . my nose was playing tricks on me. Shaking my head, I was losing it I said to myself as I ran up the stairs, two-at-a-time, to my office. Opening the top drawer, I grabbed what I needed then, rushed back down the stairs, and out the door.

Crossing Beacon Street, I entered The Commons. Strolling down the snow, shoveled walkway, I glimpsed the most gorgeous sight ever—my Sofie. She was sitting on her customary bench, wrapped in a heavy coat, gloves, scarf, and hat. My heart pounded harder and louder as I rushed to her. The gleaming smile on her face took my breath away.

I did not pull her up. Nor did I take her into my arms. I knelt in front of her, on one knee. "You aren't the only one with a special box to deliver," I said removing one of her woolen gloves and then mine to reach into my heavy-coat pocket. Pulling out a tiny square box, I looked directly into her brilliant green eyes with tears spilling from them.

"I love you, Sofie. You are the best thing that has ever happened to me in my entire life. I want you today and every day for the rest of my life. I can't bear the thought of us ever parting, again. I told you, if you ever came to Boston, I would never let you leave. I mean it, Sofie. You can never leave me. I want you forever. I want to make you my wife. The mother of my little Frog Pond dwellers. Marry me, Sofie. Go to bed with me every night. Wake up with me every day."

Nodding her head, she gave me the word I wanted to hear. "Yes, yes, yes—yes to everything."

Pulling her up from the bench, I took her into my arms and sealed the deal with our lips. Then I scooped her up, I started to walk away from the pond. "Hey, what are you doing?"

"Taking you home. I can't very well fuck you right here." I flashed her, what I hoped was, a wickedly, sexy grin.

"Put me down," she said laughing, wiggling to get out of my arms. I started to wobble, and quickly set her back down, before I dropped her on the icy ground. "I had to pull strings—well, your father did—I rented the pond for three hours. They only rent it out on Mondays. Besides, these are not my skates. Kids are being denied, so you and I could have a romantic skate. The pond is all ours."

Then it hit me. The ice was empty. I never even noticed it wasn't swarmed with people, gliding across it. Once I saw her, everything around me had disappeared. It was only Sofie I cared to see . . . to touch . . . to smell . . . to taste. All I wanted to hear was her, saying "yes" to my proposal.

Lifting my future wife back into my arms, I turned toward the cafe. Making our way, I told people as we went, "Pond open. Go get skates." Once we reached the snack shack, I informed the manager that kids were to skate free, on me, and made all the necessary arrangements. Then I stocked back to Sofie's bench, still carrying her. Setting her next to me, I put on my skates, explaining as I tied them up. "Here's the deal. We skate for an hour or less. Depending on how long I can touch you without really touching you. Then I take you to our home. By the way, where are you staying? How did you know my skate size?"

"Well..." she hesitated, leaning her head on my shoulder, laughing.

Then she looked up at me with her big green eyes. "Do you have something else up your sleeve, future Mrs. Blaxton?"

"Mmmm... I like the sound of that."

"I love it—now, tell me—what other surprises you

have in store for me?"

She stood up, smiling, extending her gloved hand out to me. "Skate with me first, then, I will tell you . . . and show you." The grin on her face was killing me.

"Hmm… one hour!"

"One hour," she repeated, pulling me along. I followed her out to the ice to join our ice skating guests.

Holding her hand tightly, we took several trips around the ice. I showed her some of my fancy skating. I got a few twirls out of her. Who knew a California girl could ice skate? I watched her, aching to have more of her. "Sofie, your hour is up," I informed her. She smiled. "I can't take anymore. I need you alone. All to myself." I guided her around the ice, to the skate rental shack, exchanging her shoes, and settling my rental tab. Then I scooped her up in my arms. There was no stopping me.

"Put me down. I can walk," she weakly protested with her arms, tight around my neck.

"No, the best day of my life, I carried you home. I intend to do it again, now." I walked briskly around the pond, up the sidewalk, across the street, to our front door. Unlocking it, we entered. Then I kicked it shut, locked it, and proceeded right up the stairs like the day I first brought her home. Only this time, once I had her undressed, there was no waiting. I attacked her mouth, her neck, her breasts, her sex, and then, I sunk deep inside of her. Filling her over and over, making her purr my name. She was finally home. I was never ever saying goodbye to her ever again.

Epilogue

THREE YEARS LATER...

SUMMERTIME HAD ROLLED around. The sun and blue skies had called to me, asking me to join them in The Commons, again. I smiled as I sat on the edge of the pond with my toes in the water, watching the little ones frolic. I loved the tiny voices, especially the one closest to me. "Look! Here comes Daddy!" squealed a little ice cream covered mouth. Raising my head, I saw a gorgeous man, wearing a tailored suit, walking our way, carrying a picnic basket. I understood her excited outburst, I squealed inside every time I saw him, too.

Setting down the picnic basket, a dark-haired toddler with pigtails and lavender eyes wrapped her two sticky arms around his leg. He immediately reached down, pulled her into his arms, rubbed noses with her, and then bent over to place a kiss on my lips. "Eww," giggled Autumn, causing us both to laugh.

"What do you mean eww? I love mommy. I like to kiss her." He tickled her. She giggled. I smiled as he helped me up. "Lunch for my girls…"

"Don't forget brother," she said, squirming to get

down.

"Of course, how could I forget?" Drake said reaching over and rubbing my very round belly.

AS THE SEASONS changed, so did our life…

A few weeks before Drake proposed, I had begun to pack up my belongings, mainly clothes and some personal keepsakes. I had put my bungalow on the real estate market as soon as I secured the position with Drake's architectural firm. I began shipping my things to Boston, most items in my house, I left. The new owner would have the option of keeping the furnishings. Everything I wanted was already housed in a townhouse on Beacon Street.

When I was making these decisions, I turned to David. Talking over my plans, including another film he was going to be filming in a year and a half. I said I was on board as long as Drake and I could work as a team. In fact, I had decided that that was the only way I would ever work as a production designer, in the future. I was firm. I wanted Drake. Luckily, when I told him, he loved the idea—we worked well as a team on projects together. It was no longer his dream job or my dream job, but ours.

The night that Drake proposed, he tried to talk me into flying out the next morning to Vegas. He didn't want to wait. He wanted to be married. He wanted to start a family. As soon as possible. Unbeknownst to us, we became pregnant the night I said yes to forever with Drake.

The next morning, I thought he was going to have a heart-attack as he walked into his closet. My clothes, shoes, and his robe had all been installed. Thanks to Drake's father, Charles, and his wife, Vivian, my move to Boston was a breeze. They had invited me into their home to stay while I got everything lined up. Once my belongings arrived, Charles stored my items in his warehouse. The day I had arranged to surprise Drake, Charles had everything moved into my new permanent home. He also, assured me that I wasn't jumping the gun. His son had poured his heart out to him. I was all he wanted. He loved me. Also, he knew that Drake had long ago purchased an engagement ring for me through his auction house—before he came to LA. That shocked me.

However, I really shocked the hell out of my man when I insisted on accompanying him to work. He stopped dead in his tracks when people on the crew knew me by name. My move-in surprise was nothing compared to this. Staring at me, I grinned back at him. "Show me the theatre; I'm dying to see it in person."

"My pleasure." With a quizzical look on his gorgeous face, he studied me with his penetrating lavender eyes. I tried not to laugh. "Sofie…"

"Yes, boss!" I exclaimed, beaming at him.

"You? You are the theatre expert that Patrick hired?"

I nodded, letting it all sink in. "You are the person I have been emailing with for the last two months?" I laughed with another nod. "This is the project you were so thrilled to be part of . . . my dream?

"Yes, to all of the above. I'm here to make your dream a reality."

"In more ways than you could ever imagine."

"Are you happy?"

"Am I happy? A huge smile painted his beautiful face. Then he picked me up and spun me around. I laughed. I have to admit, I was giddy. Then, I was delighted when he settled me on my feet to give me an earth-shattering kiss. Delicious. "I'm always happy when I'm in charge, when I can control you."

"Is that so? Does this mean that you will be showing me who is in charge on this job site?" I asked, tossing a sassy wink in his direction.

"Most definitely," was his answer. Not only did he stand behind that statement, but on multiple occasions. Over and over, he made his point. Working, as well as, playing together, suited us perfectly.

Breaking from work for a week at the end of April, we made our way to the Cape to get married. Very small and intimate with limited family and a few friends. Charles and Vivian opened their house to my parents, Gracee, David, Nelle, and their little bundle, Oscar, of course. David served as Drake's best man and Gracee was my maid of honor, still not talking about her mystery man. My father walked me down the aisle to my husband-to-be. We opted for a shoeless, short and simple ceremony on the beach, next to a sandcastle built by my groom, early that morning. We both dressed casually; Drake in tan linen pants with a white, long-sleeved, muslin shirt and I wore a white slip dress that showed off my little bump.

After saying our "I dos," and kissing for the first time as Mr. and Mrs. Drake Blaxton, we treated our guest to a catered feast, on the patio. Other attendees to our wedding included a few partners from Drake's firm, such as Patrick and his wife, and Marco brought Kimee. Lila sent her regrets; she, we later learned, was out of the country, working on a film with Blaine. The evening was magical, complete with twinkling lights, streaming romantic music, dancing in the arms of the love of life, and feeling our baby kick for the first time.

We were thrilled to hear we were having a healthy, baby girl. Drake set right to work, designing an amazing nursery. Of course, he had planned way beyond infancy. Our princess had her own pink, theatrical oasis, complete with a stage, a dress up area with a variety of costumes. Autumn loved her room. He had done a spectacular job.

This time around, as soon as we knew we were expecting a boy, a whole new theme was brewing in the mind of Drake. A cityscape was quickly constructed in the room that linked to Autumn's with a Jack and Jill bathroom between. Drake really out did himself, again. He had city murals painted on the walls and then building models were scattered about the room. A double train track was installed around the top of the room. The floor featured roadway rugs, perfect for the abundant of cars and trucks that were ready to be played with, when the baby turned into a toddler. Our son's room was a mini city. I was sure he would be just as delighted with his room as he grew into it.

He would be arriving soon. We still hadn't decided on his name. Not like Autumn. That was easy, she was born on the first day of the Fall season. Not to mention, it is truly my. . . our favorite time of the year. Perfect name for our favorite little girl.

LOOKING OVER AT Drake spread out on our picnic blanket, shoes and jacket off, sleeves rolled up, he took my breath away. So handsome... I loved the laughter from Autumn as she fed him grapes. My heart melted. I was living my true dream. Awakening every morning to my man, enjoying our own Frog Pond dweller, expecting another one any day. What could be better? Nothing.

THE END

AWAKENING TO YOU TRILOGY PLAYLIST...

Please Come To Me Boston – Dave Loggins

Who'd Have Known – Lily Allen

Let Her Go – Passenger

Stay With Me – Sam Smith

Just Like Heaven – Katie Melua

Boston – Augustana

Falling In – Lifehouse

Not Over – Daughtry

Come Home – One Republic

All I need – Christina Aguilera

Home – Phillip Phillips

OTHER BOOKS BY FIFI FLOWERS

A Window to Love, (Book 1, Windows Series)

Reclining Nude in Chicago,
(Book 1, Encounters Series)

A WINDOW TO LOVE, (BOOK 1, WINDOWS SERIES)

Melissa Bennette, a young beautiful woman who has tragically lost her parents in a devastating plane crash, is set to spend another Christmas holiday alone until one night as she gazes into the dressed up holiday windows of New York City and her path crosses with the gorgeous man of her dreams.

Evan Duke is the world's top male model, dreamed about and wanted by women everywhere, but he only has eyes for her.

This erotic tale of twists, turns and surprises stretches from twinkling lights of New York to the sun drenched beaches of Santa Monica to the art world of Paris. With each destination, the layers of their lives and closely held secrets fall away as a beautiful love grows out of the weeds of self doubt and heartbreak.

This book contains sexually explicit material and is intended for adult readers only.

A Window to Love,
(Book 1, Windows Series)
available…

RECLINING NUDE IN CHICAGO, (BOOK 1, ENCOUNTER SERIES)

What Happens when freelance art writer Julia Van Rothfelder is mistaken for an artist's life model and finds herself reclining nude in Chicago?

"Reclining Nude in Chicago" is book one of a new Encounters series by Fifi Flowers... Several standalone novellas featuring business women who travel and enjoy interesting encounters.

This book contains sexually explicit material and is intended for adult readers only

Reclining Nude in Chicago,
(Book 1, Encounter Series)
available...

AWAKENING TO YOU... TRILOGY

Sofie James is a successful set designer, trying to break into the male dominated production design realm and lacking any personal obligations she sees a clear path to success.

Drake Blaxton is a senior partner in an architectural firm who has always been focused and grounded in his career while completely noncommittal in his personal life.

A chance encounter at their favorite pond.

A fateful storm that could change everything.

What happens when Sofie and Drake's worlds collide into each other, awakening a thundering passion that neither were ever open to having?

This book contains sexually explicit material and is intended for adult readers only

ABOUT THE AUTHOR

While daydreaming of her time spent sipping cafe creme in the cafes of Paris, Fifi Flowers, an internationally known artist turn author from the Los Angeles area of California, writes romance novels and paints fantasies with a Parisian flair.

FOR THE LATEST
FIFI FLOWERS BOOK NEWS...

Twitter:
@FifiFlowers

Facebook:
https://www.facebook.com/OfficialFifiFlowers

Goodreads:
http://www.goodreads.com/FifiFlowers

Email:
Fifi@atelierdefififlowers.com

Official Fifi Flowers website:
https://www.FifiFlowers.com

Printed in Great Britain
by Amazon